THE SPIDER:
SCOURGE OF THE YELLOW FANGS

THE **MASTER OF MEN !**

SPIDER®

SCOURGE OF THE YELLOW FANGS

By Grant Stockbridge

STEEGER BOOKS • 2020

CHAPTER 1
THE MAN FROM SINGAPORE

RICHARD WENTWORTH lifted the speaking tube. "Slow up, Jackson," he ordered. "It's at the next corner that Charlie Wing said to wait."

Jackson, the chauffeur, nodded, and cut down the speed of the long limousine. They were riding south on the Bowery, under the Second Avenue Elevated structure. The building at the corner, which they were approaching, was a cheap lodging house that provided rooms for homeless men at twenty-five and fifty cents a night.

Drunks and derelicts were passing up and down the street in front of the lodging house, mingling with the few pedestrians who had to be abroad in this section of the city at this hour of the night.

Wentworth turned to the beautiful woman who sat beside him, and pressed her hand. Her cameo-like perfection of beauty might have impressed one as cold and hard, had it not been for the warmth of feeling that lay in her long eyes, or for the expressive curve of her lips.

Now, as she met Wentworth's glance, there seemed to lurk in the depths of those eyes a dim, haunting trace of unquiet, perhaps of worry.

"Dick!" she exclaimed throatily. "I—I can't explain it, but

The two Chinese were hurled through the door by the streams of slugs.

I'm—afraid; afraid of something I can't put a name to! Have you brought your gun?"

He smiled, tapped the slight bulge under his left armpit. "Of course, Nita. But there's little to worry about. True, Charlie Wing sounded a bit overwrought on the phone, but—"

She broke in impatiently: "Dick, I'm sure it's serious. You know these premonitions of mine—I've had the same feeling in the past, and you know that disaster has always followed. Somehow, I think that this meeting with Charlie Wing is going to lead us into—"

3

She broke off as a shrill, high-pitched scream sounded above the rumble of the elevated train overhead.

Jackson jammed on his brakes, and Wentworth, moving with the speed and precision of the experienced adventurer that he was, had pushed open the door and was out on the curb, gun in hand, almost before the limousine had come to a full stop.

The scream was repeated once more, from directly above, almost as an echo of the first shriek. And then a man's body came hurtling down out of the air.

It was whirling about, with arms and legs flailing wildly in every direction. As Wentworth stared upward with growing horror at the inevitable doom of the unfortunate man, he realized that the victim could only have fallen from the roof of the cheap lodging house before which he stood.

The body was dropping with express train speed, passing the sixth, the fifth, the fourth floors, to the accompaniment of repeated shrieks of stark fright from the falling man. And even as Wentworth stared upward, he glimpsed a sinister face peering over the cornice of the roof—a face that disappeared immediately.

Men in the street were shouting, scurrying away from the spot where the man would fall. The falling body was angling outward from the building, and as it swished past the second floor, it struck the railing of the elevated structure a glancing blow, and caromed back toward the building line.

A moment later it landed with a sickening thud just within the open doorway of the lodging house. It lay, twisted into a dreadful, impossible position.

Wentworth felt a surging attack of nausea for an instant, but he repressed it, and holstering his gun he leaped forward, knelt beside the broken thing that had been a living man only a few seconds ago. A crowd had formed, but they kept their distance, and Wentworth thought that he was alone until he glanced beside him and saw that Jackson, his chauffeur, was also there. Wentworth did not touch the body, but he gazed at the features of the dead man. He had struck the ground with the back of his head, and his skull was entirely bashed in. But, miraculously, his features were untouched, except for a peculiar livid gash in the right cheek. Those features were Chinese, but they betrayed a slight admixture of white blood. Wentworth's lips tightened grimly. He recognized the man, and so did Jackson. "It—it's Charlie Wing, sir!"

WENTWORTH DID not answer. He was prying loose from the dead man's fingers a small square of yellow paper upon which were written two columns of Chinese ideographs.

A policeman in uniform came lumbering up from somewhere, and the crowd, which still kept a respectful distance, pointed excitedly toward the doorway where they knelt.

Wentworth and Jackson got up from beside the body, giving the patrolman a view of its crushed horror.

"Holy Mother of God!" the officer exclaimed. "It's another suicide!" He bent over Charlie Wing's pitiful remains. "Why will these bums keep on knocking themselves off on my beat!"

Wentworth drew Jackson away from the body. He waved to Nita, whose white face he could see, peering out from the limousine, then spoke to the chauffeur. "Charlie didn't kill himself, of course, Jackson."

"I know that, sir," he said soberly.

"He was thrown from the roof. And the man who did it is still in this building."

Jackson's face hardened. He became taut. "What'll we do, sir? Tell the cop, or go after him ourselves?"

"Go after him ourselves. If we tell the cop we'll only succeed in getting ourselves held as material witnesses. Come on."

The two men entered the lobby, headed toward the single, wide-caged, rickety elevator. They had to push through a throng of seedy lodgers, who had congregated there, watching the scene with avid eyes. At one side of the lobby there was a makeshift desk, but the clerk was not there. Neither was the elevator operator. Both were at the entrance.

Suddenly, Wentworth uttered an exclamation. His eyes were fixed upon the stairway at the rear, behind the elevator. A man was stealthily coming down those stairs. And in the instant that he turned toward them, Wentworth knew that it was the same man whose face had peered down at him from the roof.

It was a yellow face, high-cheeked, with close-cropped hair. And the man wore the dark silken, loose-fitting garments to which many of the Chinese residents of the neighborhood still clung.

The Chinaman saw that he was observed, and sprinted down

the last few steps. Wentworth's hand moved up and down from his shoulder holster, to reappear with his automatic.

"Stop!" he shouted.

The man did not obey. Instead he reached the floor in a single leap, and ran toward a door which swung wide open at the rear.

Once more Wentworth shouted: "Stop! Stop or I'll shoot!"

The man swung around, raised his right arm. In his hand there was clearly visible the long, straight knife which he held by the tip of the blade between thumb and index finger. He was going to hurl it, and the accuracy of the Chinese hatchet-men with the throwing-knife is well known. This man handled his knife like an expert.

In a graceful, swift arc, he brought his arm forward. At the end of that arc he would release the knife, and it would sail through the air, true to its mark—in this case, Richard Wentworth's heart.

Jackson uttered an exclamation of dismay, and reached frantically for his own gun. But Wentworth stood spraddle-legged in the middle of that lobby, and raised his automatic, snapped a single shot at the Chinese hatchet-man. The explosion thundered in the enclosed lobby, deafening the ears of all those present.

The slug from the heavy forty-five crashed into the hatchet-man's arm, just above the elbow. The knife fell from suddenly nerveless fingers, clattered to the tiled floor. The Chinaman uttered a howl of pain as the impact of the bullet sent him staggering backward.

He swung, groping with his left hand for the doorway, and stumbled out.

Wentworth sprang after him.

AND JUST then, in the doorway appeared the silken-clad figures of two more hatchet-men. The pair had apparently been waiting outside for their confederate. Each was armed with a sub-machine gun, and they raised their weapons simultaneously, covering the throng in the lobby, protecting the retreat of their wounded companion.

Wentworth brought up short, facing the muzzles of those two sub-machine guns. He was very close to the two men, and he could see the tautness of the muscles of their faces. There was an unnatural wildness in their eyes that is not usually present in the eyes of the yellow races. Wentworth knew at once that these hatchet-men were under the influence of some powerful drug, that they would in all probability pull the trips of their guns before backing out. And if they did that, they would mow down dozens of those in the lobby.

This passed through Wentworth's mind in the split-second while he faced them across the short intervening space of white-tiled floor. And then his automatic was barking, with quick staccato explosions, while Jackson's gun echoed his shots. Jackson had been a sergeant in the World War, had served under Major Wentworth. And since then, those two had been inseparable in many parts of the world. Jackson had learned to think and act fast, and he could almost always guess what his master would do in a given situation. Now he reacted almost as quickly as

Wentworth, and the reverberations of his gun blended with those of Wentworth's automatic.

The two Chinese were literally hurled backward, out through the doorway, by the two steady streams of slugs. The sub-machine guns fell to the floor. Both men were dead virtually before their bodies had passed through that doorway!

Wentworth exclaimed: "Good work, Jackson!" His voice was almost drowned by the reverberating echoes of the shots as he sped through the doorway, leaping over the dead bodies of the two gunmen.

This door opened into a side street off the Bowery, and he got out just in time to see a sedan spurt away from the curb, with the wounded hatchet-man clinging to the running board.

He glimpsed a yellow face peering through the rear window, then saw the muzzle of another sub-machine gun thrust out at him. Instinctively his gun came up, and the two remaining shots thundered out with the accuracy and precision of unerring marksmanship.

The yellow face disappeared from the rear window, and the machine gun dropped to the asphalt. He had scored a perfect hit on that face. But now the fleeing car swerved around the corner, turning northward. Because he had been compelled to shoot at the machine gunner, Wentworth had been prevented from attempting to stop the flight of the car by puncturing one of its tires.

"It's gone, sir!" Jackson exclaimed bitterly. "And I didn't have a shot left. I emptied the magazine at those two killers inside!"

Wentworth was looking around desperately for a means of pursuing the fleeing car. There was nothing in sight. And just then, even before the screaming of the fleeing sedan's tires around the corner had died away, his own limousine came tearing into the street from the Bowery!

Wentworth's eyes lit up with admiration. Nita van Sloan had moved into the chauffeur's seat, and it was she who was driving it.

Nita, though born and bred in the aristocratic atmosphere of New York's elite, was herself no hot-house flower. She was a red-blooded woman, she loved Richard Wentworth, and she shared his adventures with him—whether he liked it or not. It was at her insistence tonight that he had taken her along to this meeting with Charlie Wing. She had heard the shooting around the corner, and had acted with the swift instinct of one who is used to living with the breath of danger in her nostrils.

Now, as she slewed the heavy limousine into the side street from the Bowery, she had her own small twenty-two calibre pistol in one hand. She waved to Wentworth with this hand, and veered in toward the curb, reaching over to push open the door so that he could jump in.

BUT JUST as Wentworth was about to leap forward, a hard hand gripped his sleeve, yanked him back.

"No ye don't, begorra! Ye'll stay right here till the sergeant comes!"

It was the uniformed cop. He had raced through the lobby

too late to get into the fight, but in plenty of time to keep Wentworth from joining the pursuit of the fleeing sedan.

Wentworth wrenched his sleeve free of the patrolman's grip.

"Let go, you fool!" he exclaimed. "The killers are getting away—"

He started toward the limousine, with Jackson beside him. The cop's eyes narrowed. "Is that so? Well, you just stand still, or I'll drill ye!" The patrolman had his service revolver out, and he leveled it at Jackson and Wentworth. "And you, too, young woman. Just turn off that motor, and get out. You all got a lot of explaining to do to the sergeant—"

Wentworth said out of the side of his mouth to Nita van Sloan: "Get going, Nita. For God's sake, try to get on the trail of that sedan. Your premonition was right. This is a big thing—"

He stopped speaking, and moved so that his body blocked the patrolman's view of the limousine. Nita needed no more than that hint. She already had the motor in first gear. Now she let up the clutch, stepped down hard on the gas, and the long, powerfully engined car leaped away from the curb as if it had been a missile hurled from a ballista.

The officer grew red in the face, swung away from Wentworth, with his back to Jackson, and raised his revolver, sighting carefully at the rear tire.

Wentworth winked to Jackson, who grinned, and negligently raised his arm, knocking up the officer's gun, which exploded into the air. The limousine swung to the right, around the corner, and disappeared in the direction taken by the Chinamen's sedan.

The patrolman whirled upon Jackson, swearing hoarsely. "So ye'll interfere with the law, will ye! I'll show—"

He stopped as Wentworth seized him by the shoulder, yanked him around. Wentworth's jaw was thrust out at a pugnacious angle, and his eyes were cold and bleak.

"That'll be enough of that, you fool! Don't you understand that we're only trying to aid the law? Don't you understand that the man who's lying dead out in front isn't a suicide, but was *murdered?* Don't you understand that his murderer has just escaped, and that you prevented me from going after him?"

The patrolman backed away before the cold fury in Wentworth's gaze. "By Jiminy! You don't say!"

Wentworth took a step after him. "And what's more, because of you, the woman I love has gone after those killers single-handed! If anything happens to her, by God, I'll hold you personally responsible!"

The crowd had come to the rear door of the lodging house now, and was staring at the scene, goggle-eyed, looking from the dead bodies of the two hatchet-men to the naked guns in the hands of Wentworth, Jackson and the cop. Now a siren sounded from around the corner on the Bowery. The cop exclaimed: "That'll be the headquarters car. Come on!"

Wentworth and Jackson followed him through the lodging house to the front. They arrived there just in time to see a stocky, well-built, dignified man descending from the police car.

The officer said: "It's the Commissioner himself! He's been answering all calls in Chinatown for the last week!"

WENTWORTH WENT through the front entrance, stepping carefully over the body of Charlie Wing. As he did so, he slipped into his coat pocket the small yellow square of paper which he had taken from the murdered man's hand.

That message was written in Cantonese—but Charlie Wing had known that he could read Cantonese as well as a native son of China. And though the sheet of yellow paper might be considered as a clue that should be turned over to the police, Wentworth had seen only a single one of the characters in the message; and that character spelled a name that must not be mentioned in connection with himself, yet a name that meant the message was for him alone.

That one name was: "Spider!"

The name of the Spider was hated by many, loved and revered by others. Some years ago there had appeared in the underworld a darkly mysterious personage whose seldom-seen face was a travesty of ugliness, whose figure was cloaked in a long cape, and whose two blazing automatics had meted out swift and unrelenting justice to criminals in high places.

Powerful overlords of crime had fallen before those accurate, deadly automatics; vicious and murderous organizations had been blasted wide open to the accompaniment of their deep-throated reverberations; plots that had come within an ace of success were unravelled as Alexander had unravelled the Gordian Knot—by the straight and sure shooting of the Spider.

Men speculated as to who this Spider might be. He was hunted by the underworld as a dangerous enemy who must be eliminated; and he was also hunted by the police. For his methods were unorthodox, outside the law. He did not wait

for a criminal to stand an expensive trial, to hire expensive lawyers and get away scot free; he administered his own justice in the underworld, and he was therefore proscribed by the law. Commissioner Kirkpatrick wanted to send the Spider to the electric chair as much as the underworld wanted to riddle him with bullets.

But fewer than a half dozen people in the United States knew that Richard Wentworth, wealthy young sportsman, dilettante of the arts and letters, adventurer in the far corners of the world, was also—the Spider!

Those few persons were Nita van Sloan, his fiancée; Jackson, his chauffeur; Jenkyns, his valet, who had served his father before him; and Ram Singh, his Sikh warrior servant.

In other parts of the world there was a man here, and a man there who knew Wentworth's secret. Such a one was a certain Cabinet Member in England, who might have faced a firing squad during the World War had it not been for the intervention of the Spider. Another one who knew his secret was the reigning Maharajah of Jollapore, who might have been lying with a knife in his back in some noisome gutter of Calcutta, had it not been for the Spider.

The Maharajah of Jollapore had offered the Spider a reward far greater in value than a king's ransom; but the Spider had no need of money. And so, even to this day, the Maharajah sent to

Richard Wentworth, once every year, a gift whose value cannot be calculated in dollars.*

Richard Wentworth's secret was safe with every one of these persons. Not at the price of life itself would they ever betray him.

But there was one man never allowed to become positively aware that Wentworth was the Spider. That man was the one who had just alighted from the headquarters car—Police Commissioner Stanley Kirkpatrick. The Commissioner was morally certain of the identity of the Spider. But it was a matter that neither discussed with the other; for Kirkpatrick had more than once warned his friend that if he caught the Spider he would send him to the electric chair—even if he turned out to be his own brother. Kirkpatrick was first, and above all, a loyal and courageous officer of the law.

AS HE descended from the headquarters car, he shook hands with Wentworth, raised his eyebrows questioningly as if to

---

* AUTHOR'S NOTE: One such gift is a sabre, whose hilt is encrusted with rare jewels. It had been handed down in the family of the traditional lords of Jollapore for more than five centuries. It was the original sabre worn by Tamerlane during the Mongol invasion of India. The British Museum had offered a fabulous sum for that sabre, but it was not for sale. Yet the Maharajah of Jollapore gave it freely to the Spider, and it hangs alone on a wall of the music room in Richard Wentworth's penthouse apartment on Central Park West. Not even Nita van Sloan knows the exact nature of the service which Wentworth rendered to the Maharajah to earn such generous gratitude. That secret is shared only by Ram Singh, Wentworth's Sikh servant. And Wentworth himself grows significantly reticent when the incident is mentioned.

indicate his surprise at finding him there, then he swung to the uniformed patrolman.

"Another suicide, eh?" he asked grimly.

"That's what I thought it was at first, sir," the cop replied. "But then this gentleman—" indicating Wentworth—"started shooting, and there's two more dead Chinks out in back, an' a couple more got away in a car, and this gent says the guy ain't a suicide at all, but that he was murdered!"

Kirkpatrick did not approach the dead body of Charlie Wing. Instead he frowned heavily, scowled at Wentworth. What have you got to do with all this, Dick?" he demanded. "What are you doing down here?"

Wentworth shrugged. "I was driving downtown, with Nita, when we suddenly heard a scream. I jumped out, and that man's body came hurtling down. I saw some one looking down over the cornice of the roof, so Jackson and I went after him. The man got down the stairs just as we got into the lobby, and he had a couple of boy friends waiting to aid his getaway. Jackson and I winged him and bagged the two boy friends. The murderer escaped in a sedan, and Nita followed them in my car. If it hadn't been for the officer here, I might have been able to go with her. As it is, she's after them alone."

While Wentworth was talking, two police cars pulled up to the curb. One was a precinct car, the other contained the Medical Examiner and his assistants. Two more uniformed policemen arrived, and Kirkpatrick gave them orders to clear a space around the body, to keep the crowd back.

Some one from among the onlookers shouted loudly:

16

"Commissioner! That man that's talking to you took something from the dead man's hand. I saw him do it, but I couldn't tell what it was!"

Kirkpatrick frowned at Wentworth. "What are you up to, Dick? If you know anything about this, speak up. If this is murder, and you're holding anything back, you're compounding the crime!"

Wentworth's face was blank "There's nothing I can tell you, Kirk."

"Did you take anything from the dead man's hand?"

"I haven't got a thing on me that doesn't belong to me, Kirk."

The man in the crowd who had shouted before, now called out: "He did take something. Search him!"

Kirkpatrick hesitated. "Your word is good with me, Dick. Will you tell me flatly that you didn't take anything from his hand?"

Wentworth smiled. "I'd rather you searched me, Kirk. That would satisfy the gentleman out there in the crowd—and would make you feel better too."

The Commissioner shrugged. "All right, Dick, if you won't play ball."

Wentworth opened his coat, and Kirkpatrick went through his jacket and trousers pockets, feeling of the lining, patting him all over thoroughly. Kirkpatrick had had a long and bitter schooling in police work, and he was an adept at searching a suspect. When he got through, he was sure there wasn't a thing on Wentworth that he hadn't found.

While he had been going through Wentworth's clothes, he had ordered one of the plain clothes men from the headquar-

RICHARD
WENTWORTH

ters car to do the same for Jackson. Nothing was found on the chauffeur.

Kirkpatrick frowned, looked toward the man in the crowd who had tipped him off.

"Well?"

"I tell you, he took something!"

Suddenly, Kirkpatrick's eyes gleamed. "Let's see your overcoat, Dick!"

Wentworth held his breath while Kirkpatrick went through his overcoat pockets. The Commissioner brought out the small square of yellow paper.

"What's this?"

Wentworth's heart was pounding. A message in his own pocket, addressed to the Spider would take a lot of explaining. Once the Chinese interpreter down at headquarters translated it, Kirkpatrick would bear down on him like a ton of bricks. The Commissioner apparently attached a great deal of importance to this killing; if he were convinced that Wentworth had some special knowledge about it, he would place him under arrest as a material witness—and worst of all, Wentworth would never be allowed to see that paper again, would never know what the message contained, what Charlie Wing had wanted to tell him.

All this flashed through his mind with the speed of light, while Kirkpatrick was still asking: "What's this?"

Wentworth caught Jackson's eyes on him, knew that the chauffeur was waiting as tensely as he for his answer. And the answer, like a brilliant flash of inspiration, came to his tongue as easily as the smile which he forced to his lips: "If you take it to my Chinese laundry, Kirk, they might give you some of my shirts for it!"

Kirkpatrick smiled sheepishly, eyeing the Chinese ideographs. "All right, all right!" he said hastily, and thrust the paper back in Wentworth's pocket. "Now come over here and see if you can identify the body—"

ONE OF the plainclothes men, who had just come over, interrupted. "We've already identified it, sir. It's Charlie Wing. He's got a Chinese employment agency over on Pell Street. He was mixed up in an opium smuggling racket a few years ago, and we had him down to headquarters."

"I remember it," Kirkpatrick said shortly. "Just a minute."

He took Wentworth by the elbow, said: "Come here. I want to talk to you—"

"Hold it, Kirk," Wentworth protested. "Before we get into conversation, suppose you send out an alarm for that sedan. I don't relish the idea of Nita trailing after it alone—"

"By Jove, you're right!" Kirkpatrick issued swift orders to his men, and Wentworth gave the best description he could of the gunmen's car, as well as of the killer he had wounded. "You might also have all the hospitals notified, though I don't think it likely he'll go to a public hospital to be treated. More probable that some shady medico will take care of him."

The Commissioner nodded, and drew Wentworth to one side. "Now look here, Dick. I want you to tell me everything you know about this. This thing is bigger than just a murder of an isolated Chinese. I've been answering every call to Chinatown personally for the last week or so. Word has been trickling in to me of a big, mysterious combine down here in Chinatown, that's wiping out all opposition. There's one man at the head of it, and he's a devil. The Chinese are all afraid to talk—you know how they are."

"Why do you think I know anything about it?" Wentworth countered.

"Because you weren't down here by accident tonight. You know what I think? I think you had an appointment with Charlie Wing!"

Wentworth raised his eyebrows.

Kirkpatrick went on. "I remember more about Charlie Wing than you think I do, Dick. I remember that when he was in trouble a few years ago, he was cleared through the intervention of a certain person known as the Spider. What is more logical than that he should go to the Spider when he's in trouble again?"

"What has that got to do with me, Kirk?"

The Commissioner made an impatient movement with his hands. "Let's not beat about the bush, Dick. I'm morally certain that you're the Spider, and you know that I am!"

"You want me to admit I'm the Spider? Haven't you told

me time and again that you've sworn to send the Spider to the electric chair?"

Kirkpatrick literally squirmed under Wentworth's question. "God, Dick, I don't know what I want. I need help on this case. I need it desperately. There's a man here in New York whom they call 'The Man from Singapore.' That's all I can learn about him. In the last ten days there have been fifteen murders in Chinatown. They've been kept out of the papers, or played down as much as possible. Most of them have looked like suicides, just like this one. But I'm certain, from the little information my men have brought in, that they're not suicides, and that The Man from Singapore is behind them."

Wentworth looked at him reflectively. "This begins to get interesting, Kirk. Have you any idea as to the motive—"

"No!" Kirkpatrick groaned. "But there's one thing common to all of the corpses. They have a livid mark on the cheek, just like the one on Charlie Wing over there. And an hour or two after they're dead, that mark turns whitish, and takes shape. *It takes the shape of a double set of fangs—just as if the victims had been bitten by some vicious beast!*"

"Fangs, eh!" Wentworth said reflectively. "Sounds like some tong mark—"

"It's the mark of The Man from Singapore!" Kirkpatrick broke in, tensely. "One of the victims last week lived for a couple of minutes after we found him. The only words he said were: *'The mark of The Man from Singapore!'* I've got to break this thing before it goes further. Already, the people of Chinatown are beginning to lose their faith in the white police—a faith that we've been fifteen years in building up. And once the police lose their influence in Chinatown, we'll have what we had years ago—a flare-up of tong wars, murders, riots. I'm afraid that's the ultimate purpose of The Man from Singapore, Dick!"

Wentworth stared at the Commissioner evenly. "If it's as bad as you say, Kirk, then I'll do anything you ask. What do you want me to do—admit that I'm the Spider? Will that help you?"

Kirkpatrick's eyes mirrored his misery. "If you do that, Dick, I'll have to prosecute you. You know what that would mean to me. I'd rather go to the electric chair myself, but I'd have to do it. It'd be my duty, you know."

"I know, Kirk," Wentworth said drily.

"And I wouldn't want it that way. We're talking frankly now, off the record. There are a lot of things about the Spider that I admire; but he's violated the law, and he's earned the extreme penalty. Dick—I—I don't want to—send you—to the chair." Impulsively, the Commissioner put a hand on Wentworth's arm. "The Spider has helped me in the past—without my asking for it, and in his own way. Maybe the Spider would help me in this. I—I'd be willing to call a truce with him—temporarily—if he'd promise to use orthodox, legal methods; with the understanding that after this case is over, the hunt would be on again!"

For a long moment Wentworth was silent. Then: "Orthodox, legal methods!" he mused. "That would mean that the Spider would have to gather definite, legal proof against a criminal— proof that would stand up in a court of law."

"That's right. And he'd have to turn his evidence *and* the

criminal over to the police, instead of inflicting his own brand of justice!"

Wentworth's eyes gleamed. "It would be a new experience for the Spider, I suppose, to be entirely within the law." He paused, as if debating a question, then: "I think, Kirk, that you might very well count on the help of the Spider!"

Kirkpatrick breathed a sigh of relief. "Let's shake on it, Dick!" he breathed.

The two men clasped hands, and their eyes met in an unspoken pledge of loyalty. Abruptly Wentworth swung away. "I've got to go, Kirk. Lots of things to take care of!"

He motioned to Jackson, who had been watching him anxiously, and started down the Bowery toward Chinatown. Kirkpatrick watched him for a while. There was a peculiar light in his eyes....

CHAPTER 2
THE WHITE WOMAN

WENTWORTH HURRIED Jackson down the Bowery, and turned the next corner. As soon as they were out of sight of the crowd around the lodging house, Wentworth drew out the small square of yellow paper upon which Charlie Wing had written his death message.

Jackson, having served with Wentworth for three years in the interior of China, could read the Oriental ideographs as well as his master, and he peered over Wentworth's shoulder to decipher the strange script. It read as follows:

Spider *san:* Once you helped this unworthy servant. Now this unworthy servant will repay the Spider. For Charlie Wing there is no longer hope, for I am watched. They will not let me live to talk with my honorable friend. I write this while they close in on me. Spider, a wicked man is here to do ill to your country. He is The Man from Singapore. His mark is already upon many of my countrymen, and will soon be upon those of your own race. Seek him in the Eating Place of Mow Loo Fen—but be careful for he is dangerous and....

The note was broken off in the middle, as if Charlie Wing had not had time to finish.

Wentworth said bitterly: "They got him while he was writing it, Jackson. He must have taken a room upstairs. If we had come twenty minutes sooner—"

He broke off, his eyes narrowing. *"The Eating Place of Mow Loo Fen!* Do you remember the place, Jackson—on Doyers Street? It used to be the headquarters of the smuggling gang that we broke up, when Charlie Wing was involved. He was part owner of the place, and that's how the police came to suspect him."

"I remember, sir," Jackson said soberly. "The place had dozens of secret rooms, and hidden passageways. We were both almost killed. There was a trapdoor that opened under my feet, with the sewer underneath—and a live cobra waiting—"

"That's right, Jackson. And this Man from Singapore seems to have chosen it for headquarters."

"Shall we tell the police, sir? A raid—"

Wentworth laughed shortly. "You know how much good that would do! Last month, when Kirkpatrick raided Kesten's

Sanatorium, he wasn't able to find a thing there. And Kesten's was only a child's toy compared with the maze of labyrinth under Mow Loo Fen's place. No, Jackson, we've got to work under cover. We've got to find out who this Man from Singapore really is. But first, we'll phone Ram Singh,  at home. Perhaps Nita has called him. I hope to God those killers didn't spot her trailing them!"

They walked two blocks through the dingy tenement district before finding a stationery store that boasted a telephone sign outside. Wentworth was really worried. There was one thing he had held back from Nita—one thing about Charlie Wing that she did not know.

She was under the impression that Charlie had phoned to Richard Wentworth for the appointment down here on the Bowery. That was only partly true. Wentworth had an office on Broadway, run by an ex-bookmaker named Ben Laskar. It was known throughout the underworld that Laskar was the Spider's contact man, and it was to Laskar that Charlie Wing had phoned, asking for the appointment. Wentworth hadn't told Nita that, because he knew she would oppose his going. Nita didn't want the Spider to walk again. She wanted Wentworth to give all that up, to forget that he had ever been a dual personality.

"I'm tired of it all, Dick," she had said only this morning. "I'm tired of this everlasting caution, this living in a fortress, this constant worry about you. If you love me, Dick, you'll give it up, bury the Spider forever!"

She came into his arms, with her lips close to his. "If you want me, Dick," she breathed, "take me now. Let's be married at once. I—I *won't* share you with the Spider any longer! We'll go on that trip to Europe next week—you and I, alone, away from the sordidness of crime, away from the deadly danger you've been courting all these years. Court me, Dick, instead of courting danger!"

Wentworth's smile was a happy one. "We'll be married tomorrow, darling. And we'll sail Monday—Venice, the Bay of Naples, Tunis, Algiers—we'll visit them all together—"

"But you must promise me one thing, Dick—that the Spider will never walk again. Bury that cape and hat of the Spider's in some deep, inaccessible place; pack away those automatics. Be Richard Wentworth again—for always!"

"I promise, darling," he breathed. "We'll be married tomorrow—and tomorrow the Spider will cease to exist!"

That was in the morning, in Nita's apartment over the breakfast table. Wentworth had been busy that morning, and well into the afternoon, booking passage, making last minute arrangements.

And it was in the evening, just after dinner, that Ben Laskar reported Charlie Wing's call for the Spider.

Wentworth was torn between his love for Nita and the nostalgic thrill of mystery and danger. He had told Nita that Spider would cease to exist *tomorrow*. Today, the Spider could still keep an appointment. He was to meet Nita that same evening. He would have to take her along. But if she knew he went as the Spider, she would object. So he let her think that it was more or less a friendly appointment.

But Nita had sensed danger in the limousine, with that infallible instinct of hers. And in a pinch, she had risen to the occasion, just as if she were not to be married tomorrow, just as if she were not supposed to be looking forward to leaving all this behind her. Wentworth smiled tenderly as he thought of it. Perhaps the thrill of danger and excitement had gotten into her blood too, as it had in his. Perhaps he would not have such a hard job convincing Nita that they ought to stay and fight this Man from Singapore!

Jackson, walking behind him through the drab tenement district, read his mind. "Will you be wanting me to cancel that passage for you, sir?"

Wentworth threw him a side glance. Jackson understood him well. Jackson knew that he could no more resist the lure of a battle of wits against a powerful criminal antagonist than an opium user could resist the call of the poppy.

"We'll see!" he said shortly. "Right now, I want to call the apartment, and find out if Nita has called in!"

HE ENTERED the phone booth, dialed the private number of his penthouse apartment. Ram Singh, his Sikh servant, answered.

"Yes, master, the *memsahib* phoned. She related to me what has happened at the lodging house on the Bowery. She followed the car of the swine who killed your friend, and saw them enter an alley in Chinatown. She investigated, and found that the alley led to the rear of a restaurant on Doyers Street. The *memsahib* instructed me to tell you that she will be in the restaurant, and that you should go there—"

"Quick, Ram Singh!" Wentworth interrupted. "What is the name of the restaurant?"

"It is one that we know of, master—The Eating Place of Mow Loo Fen!"

Wentworth gripped the receiver tensely. This was speedy confirmation of the information in Charlie Wing's note. And Nita was there alone. If The Man from Singapore was as clever as Kirkpatrick had hinted, then Nita's life was in peril.

"Stay at the phone, Ram Singh!" he barked. "And prepare for action!"

The Sikh's deep, booming voice rolled out from the phone: "Action! The word is sweet in my ears. Praise to Allah—and I thought that the master was becoming soft!"

Wentworth hung up and joined Jackson. "Get a cab!" he snapped. "Nita's at Mow Loo Fen's. She followed the Chinese there!"

They found a taxi at the next corner, and Jackson gave the address. They were not far from Doyers Street, and it took only a few minutes to get there.

The Eating Place of Mow Loo Fen was one flight up, in a narrow four-story building in the heart of teeming Doyers Street. It was one of the many places typical of Chinatown, that furnish a point of interest for the "rubberneck busses" which conduct tours of visitors from the hinterland.

An ornate electric sign above the narrow doorway announced

the name of the place in English, and alongside it there were the Chinese characters spelling the same name. Dozens of shuffling yellow men were passing up and down the street, and at the corner were a pair of uniformed officers. Wentworth's mind ran back twenty years to the days of the tong wars in New York, when the Hip Sings battled the warriors of the On Leong Tong, and there were daily riots, and police dared not patrol the streets of Chinatown unless they walked in pairs.

A sing-song voice called out: "More knives!"

Then the streets of the lower city literally ran with blood, and the blasting of guns might have been heard at any hour of the day or night. Then men slunk through the darkness in

Chinatown, not knowing which moment might bring a knife or a bullet in the back. Hatchet-men waited in doorways and alleys for their victims, and dealt out death in the name of their ancestors and for the honor of their tongs.

Now, with the appearance of the sinister Man from Singapore, the conditions of the old days gave signs of arising once more. One of the first measures of a man who desired to cause the old tong enmities to flame once more would be to bring about a number of murders in Chinatown. That would surely destroy the faith of the resident in the police as Kirkpatrick had pointed out—and they would turn again to the protection of their tongs. Even now, the Chinese secret societies might be meeting, holding councils of war, debating the causes of the death of some of their number. There would surely be some present at those meetings who would suggest that a rival tong had instigated the murders; and the elders would turn to thoughts of vengeance.

Wentworth had that peculiar faculty of putting himself in another man's place, of thinking the thoughts that a criminal might think in a given situation. And with what little information Kirkpatrick had vouchsafed him, Wentworth was already imagining what he would do were he this mysterious Man from Singapore.

HE ALIGHTED from the taxi, and said to Jackson: "Drive around to the rear. Wait there. If for any reason, I should have to make a quick getaway, I'll find the alley. If you locate the limousine, take that; otherwise, keep the cab."

Jackson drew Wentworth aside. "I wonder if it's wise, sir,

for you to show yourself here as Mr. Wentworth. Whoever murdered Charlie Wing must have known that he was waiting to meet the Spider. They deliberately arranged for his body to come tumbling down in front of the Spider when he arrived. So now they must guess that you *are*—"

Wentworth shook his head. "I don't think they knew Charlie Wing had an appointment with anyone, Jackson. They were going to kill him, and they did kill him where they found him. The gruesomeness of his death was not for the purpose of impressing the Spider; it was for the purpose of impressing others in Chinatown with the power of the Man from Singapore. If they had known he was going to meet anyone, they would have searched him for a possible message—and have found the yellow note."

Jackson was dubious. "Nevertheless, sir, I don't think it wise for you to show yourself here. Why not go home first, get into some different clothes, put on a little make-up—"

"And leave Nita waiting here?" Wentworth scoffed. "Not—"

He broke off, staring at two men who had just approached the doorway of the Eating Place of Mow Loo Fen. One of them was tall, easily five feet ten, light complexioned, and extraordinarily broad-shouldered. He was attired in a Chesterfield and derby and spats, and he carried a heavy, silver-knobbed walking stick. His face was molded in hard, unyielding lines which were accentuated by the gray coldness of his eyes.

His companion was shorter, though still a good five feet eight, and much younger. He too wore a Chesterfield and derby, but he was slender, with a callow, uneasy expression on his features.

He could not have been more than twenty-three or twenty-four at the most.

Both men were walking swiftly, as if they were fearful of being late. Had they looked around they would have seen Wentworth, but they were too intent on reaching the entrance to the restaurant.

Wentworth seized Jackson's arm. "You recognize the big one?" he demanded.

"I should say so, sir! That's Nils Bishop! We met him in Istanbul in 1923. He was a spy for the Italians then, but later on he sold out to the Russians, and betrayed his Italian employers. Then the Turks caught him, and he was sentenced to be shot, but he sold out both the Russians and the Italians to the Turks, and the Turks let him escape. He'd betray his own brother for profit!"

"Good memory, Jackson!" Wentworth praised. He watched the two men enter Mow Loo Fen's, saw them disappear into the narrow hallway. "And the young fellow with him—he's in strange company. That young man's pictures are in the rotogravure sections every other Sunday. He's Martin Custer, the son of Frank Custer, president of the Custer Gold Refining Company!"

"That's funny, sir. What would the son of a multimillionaire be doing down here in Chinatown with a reprobate like Nils Bishop?"

Wentworth's eyes narrowed. "I'm more interested in why they're coming to Mow Loo Fen's. It can't be pleasure, to judge from the glimpse we got of their faces. Bishop was grim, and young Custer was half scared to death—if he was anything. Now go ahead, Jackson. I'll wait till you pull away in the cab before going in."

Jackson was reluctant to leave. "Perhaps I ought to go in with you, sir. Two guns are better than one in a pinch—"

Wentworth shook his head. "No good, Jackson. I'm in evening clothes, and you're wearing a chauffeur's uniform. Already I'm afraid we're attracting too much attention. That old woman over there—" he nodded in the direction of a tattered old hag who stood about twenty feet away, with a basket of gardenias under her arm—"that flower woman has been watching us. When we arrived she moved away and disappeared into one of the buildings down the street. Now she's back, and watching us again. You better go ahead, Jackson."

The chauffeur saluted stiffly. "Very well, sir!" He got back into the cab, directed the cabby to drive around the block.

As soon as the taxi pulled away, Wentworth moved toward the doorway of Mow Loo Fen's. He had hardly taken a step before he was aware of a sudden bustling in the passing crowds of yellow men about him. One man jostled him, another stepped directly in front of him, blocking his advance. He was aware that attention was suddenly centered upon him.

INSTINCTIVELY, ALL of Wentworth's senses became alert. His body grew taut, ready to repel attack from whatever quarter it came. He had been in dangerous predicaments so often in the past that he reacted almost automatically to the imminence of danger.

Now, he was conscious of swift movement behind him, while the man in front still moved awkwardly in such manner as to keep him from advancing. On either side, too, he was strangely hemmed in by smelly, yellow figures.

Acting with the swift sureness of a trained fighting machine, he whirled, with his elbows far out on either side of him, thrusting the hemming bodies away. As he turned, his eyes caught the flash of a blade glittering under the light from the street lamp a few feet away. The blade slithered through the air, propelled by a gnarled yellow hand. It was descending in a vicious thrust that would have caught him in the back just above the kidney.

Wentworth twisted quickly, his supple body swaying slightly forward. The descending blade missed his back by a scant fraction of an inch, swishing past with the vicious hiss of a striking serpent. There was a grunt of disappointment, and Wentworth raised his right elbow, thrust out with it savagely at the face of the yellow man who had wielded the knife.

He felt the bone of his elbow strike forcefully against soft cartilage, and there was a groan of pain, followed by a squeal. The knife man fell backward, dropping the blade, raising both hands swiftly to his pain-wracked, broken nose.

A sing-song voice somewhere in the darkness called out in Cantonese; "More knives! Kill him! He must not escape!"

The shadowy figures about him closed in with a swift rush. Gleaming knives appeared from capacious sleeves, flashed upward.

Wentworth's right hand streaked in and out from his shoulder holster and he was gripping his automatic. He swung it in a swishing circle about him, and the butt struck a wrist, brought a cry of pain, and sent a knife spinning into the air. Another blade came straight at his face, and he twisted back into the crowd behind him, caught the arm that drove that knife in his left hand, gripped hard and threw the weight of his body upon the grip. At the same time he jabbed his fisted automatic into the face of the one he held. The barrel smashed lips into pulp, broke teeth.

Wentworth released his hold, flailed out with both fists, fighting cannily, without panic. In his lifetime he had been in waterfront brawls in Toulon and in Algeciras; he had defended himself against belaying pins in the hands of drug-crazed pirates in the China Seas; he had fought against brass knuckles, and against the deadly garrote of the Thuggees of the Orient. He was no novice at fighting with fist or gun or knife. And if these men had thought to find an easy victim to their concerted attack, they were meeting with an unpleasant surprise. Wentworth knew all the tricks that these yellow men knew, and a few more in addition. He hurled his hundred and eighty pounds of bone and sinew at one of his remaining attackers, sent the man spinning into his companions, then reached out, seized him by the front of his coat and yanked his body toward him. A blow on the temple caused the fellow to sag, unconscious in Wentworth's grip; then Wentworth held the man in front of him for protection against knife thrusts, and lashed out with his right at those beyond. Again and again his gun barrel struck bone, brought grunts and curses.

Abruptly there came the sound of a police whistle, as the

two uniformed patrolmen from the corner came running. And as suddenly as they had appeared, the attackers faded away into the night, and the scene of violence subsided into quiet.

Yellow loiterers had formed a ring around the combat, and now, as the policemen tried to push through, Wentworth took advantage of the fact that he had not yet been seen by them. He stooped swiftly, recovered his top hat, which had fallen to the sidewalk and was a bit crushed. He placed it on his head at a jaunty angle, and slipped quickly into the dark entrance of Mow Loo Fen's place.

THERE WAS no light here, but there was a single bulb, high up at the head of the stairs, which threw a feeble glow down into the vestibule. He could hear the angry voices of the cops demanding to know what had been going on outside, and he could hear the chattering of dozens of Chinese voices, engaged in blandly telling the patrolmen nothing at all. He was as safe from pursuit and questioning by those policemen as if he were invisible; for the Chinese would never tell the white policemen what had happened. They would jabber away for many minutes, until the cops grew disgusted and went away.

Wentworth was breathing a bit quickly from his exertion. Swiftly he ran his fingers up and down his coat and trousers, to make sure his clothing had not been slashed by the knives of the attackers; then he smoothed out his hat as best he could, started toward the stairs.

His lips were set grimly, and his eyes glowed in the darkness with a new sense of excitement. Here was battle, thrill, danger indeed. The enemy—whoever he was—had struck swiftly, surely, ruthlessly. No doubt about it, Wentworth had been observed, had been watched even while he talked to Kirkpatrick. He must have been followed down here to Chinatown, must have been observed from some vantage point. It was significant of the type of organization controlled by this Man from Singapore—if indeed it was he who had instigated the attack—that he could so quickly dispose his forces to launch the attack. And it was doubly significant of the character of the Man from Singapore that he had decided in a moment that Wentworth was dangerous to him and must be eliminated without delay.

Wentworth gloried in a battle with a worthy antagonist. And here was one who could be counted upon for the unexpected. Now Wentworth was convinced that other attempts would be made—perhaps the fertile brain of this mysterious Man from Singapore was already planning another attack upstairs-

Suddenly with his foot upon the first step, and with the shouts of the crowd outside still dinning in his ears, Wentworth tensed, and a cold chill tingled along his shoulder blades.

He was aware of another presence in the dark hallway!

He suddenly sensed movement, heard the sibilant intake of breath of a person close to him.

Wentworth was no man to wait supinely for an attack. He lunged forward in the direction where he sensed the presence to be, his left arm covering his throat against a knife thrust, his right groping for what it might find. He found the cloth of a coat, gripped it, and would have smashed down with his left fist at where he thought the face to be, had it not been for the sibilant whisper that came from the other.

"Wait, Spider!"

Those two words were spoken in a woman's voice.

Those two words, uttered there in the darkness of the hallway of Mow Loo Fen's Eating Place, told Wentworth much. *They told him that he was known as the Spider.* They told him that this fight against the Man from Singapore must be made by him in the open, against an unseen and unknown antagonist. They told him that all the advantage would be on the other side this time, and that he must battle against higher odds than he had reckoned. Jackson had been right in figuring that the enemy would assume him to be the Spider.

The fact that these thoughts flashed through his mind did not interfere with the swift sureness of his movements. Even while the woman spoke in the darkness, his small fountain pen flashlight was out of his overcoat pocket, and he sent a stabbing ray of light in her direction, still holding on to the coat he had gripped.

The face and figure that the tiny beam of light disclosed caused an exclamation to rise to his lips, which he barely managed to restrain.

IT WAS the old flower woman he had noticed out in the street a few moments ago. She was bundled in her coat, which was a thing of tattered patches. And under the coat he could see that she wore a heavy black sweater. Her hat, a relic of the early Nineteen-Twenties, was torn, moth-eaten.

And the face of her was ageless as time itself, ravaged by disease and want and cold and hunger and drugs. Lackluster lips that curled back upon gumless teeth, sunken cheeks and eyes that sat deep in cavernous sockets bespoke the hell this woman must have lived through. The basket of gardenias still rested in the crook of her left elbow, and her right hand was raised as if to fend off a blow.

Outside, the police were still arguing with the sullen Chinese. At any moment they might think of looking in here, and Wentworth did not want to be found, questioned. Yet he was held by the sudden flow of words from the old hag's lips.

"Spider! I am your friend! Beware of the Man from Singapore. He will try and try until he kills you!"

Wentworth slowly released his grip on her coat. He clicked off the flashlight. "Why do you call me Spider?" he asked.

"Never mind why. I *know.* Listen closely, Spider, for I must speak quickly and be gone. Charlie Wing tried to tell you something, but he died too soon. He wanted your help, but not for himself. Will you avenge his death?"

Swift conjecture raced through Wentworth's mind. He guessed now why the old hag called him Spider. If she knew of Charlie Wing's death, she must have been present at the Bowery lodging house when he was thrown from the roof. She had known that Charlie was going to meet the Spider, had seen Wentworth arrive at that moment, and had put two and two together.

Bitterly Wentworth cursed the impulse that had made him take Nita along for that appointment. Had it not been for her, he would have gone as the Spider and not as Wentworth, would have avoided this exposure. This old hag might be a friend, and then again she might be another emissary of the Man from Singapore, sent to make sure that he was the Spider. He doubted the latter conjecture, for the Man from Singapore would hardly have planned this test if he had planned to kill Wentworth before he could enter. The chances were that the woman was sincere, that she really was a friend, had been in the confidence of Charlie Wing. Her voice belied her appearance. It bespoke culture of a sort, even though that culture was overlaid by a film of coarseness that must have been acquired in the slums of the city. Everything was in her favor, yet Wentworth dared not admit in so many words that he was the Spider.

The woman took his silence for permission to go on.

"You will not find the trail to the Man from Singapore upstairs. It is too well covered there. But Charlie Wing could have told you much, and I know all that Charlie knew—and more. I will help you, I will tell you how to trap the Man from Singapore. Come to my room tomorrow, and I will tell you all you need to know. I live in the rear house, behind the *lychee* nut shop of Sin Foo, two doors down. I'm on the third floor, in the rear. There are eight rooms on the floor, but my door will have a little circle marked on the panel, so that you will know it. *Do not fail to come!*"

"Why do you do this?" Wentworth demanded. "And why should I trust you?"

The old woman laughed harshly. "I have reasons. Here is one of them. Put on your flashlight again!"

Wentworth obeyed, clicked on the little light.

"Look!" the woman breathed, blinking under the light.

With shaking fingers she tore open her coat, and the sweater beneath, tore at the front of her dress. The material ripped, revealing a shriveled breast. Her skin was strangely white, far different from that of her face. But upon that white skin there appeared an ugly, livid mark—for all the world like the mark of the fangs of some beast of prey—two tusks and three stumps between.

Wentworth gasped. This was a white woman. And upon her body was the same mark that Kirkpatrick had told him was found upon the dead bodies of the murdered Chinese.

The woman suddenly closed her coat. "That," she whispered, "is the mark of the Man from Singapore. I would gladly die, if it would help to destroy him, to save others from this mark. Believe me, Spider—and come tomorrow, without fail!"

And he heard her shuffle away in the darkness, not out into the street, *but back toward the rear of the hallway!*

Her awkward footsteps grew less and less distinct, and then died out altogether. Wentworth made a mental note of the fact—there must be some method of egress from the building behind the stairway—*or else the woman was in league with the occupants of the building!*

CHAPTER 3
FANGS OF FATE

T HE STRAINS of Oriental music were drifting down from above as Wentworth mounted the stairs. On the first floor a quiet, dimly lit corridor seemed impregnated with the mingled odors of food and mustiness. He glanced around curiously, cautiously. It was a long time since he had been here, but he noted with quick interest that some changes had been made.

Formerly, the main dining room had extended all the way to the head of the stairs. Now, there was this corridor, and a door at the far end, which was a few inches ajar. Light streamed out through the opening, and the sounds of music were stronger. They had changed from the plaintive Oriental tune to a lively swing-time piece. Wentworth thought it strange that there was not an attendant here. Perhaps that functionary had been removed for the time being, while the attack in the street had been launched. Or perhaps the stage was set here for another attempt, in case the first one failed.

It would not do to underrate this antagonist. From what had occurred so far, it was fully conceivable that the Man from Singapore would be a good enough general to organize a second line of attack.

Wentworth moved cautiously down the corridor, all his senses alert. But nothing happened.

As he approached the door, it was suddenly opened by a smiling bowing, chubby little Chinaman who wore horn-rimmed glasses. He was garbed in an embroidered silken jacket with wide sleeves, and his hands were thrust into those sleeves.

"Welcome to the Eating Place of Mow Loo Fen. In the name of my master I bid you welcome. All in this humble place is at the disposal of the honorable guest!"

One might have thought, from the smiling, subservient attitude of this Chinaman, that no knives had ever flashed in the darkness of the street below, that no old woman had just torn open her dress to show upon her breast the livid mark of the yellow fangs, the signature of the Man from Singapore.

It was this quality of blandness in the Chinese that was so disarming to the white men coming in contact with them. Wentworth had learned in a bitter school that white men are only children by comparison with the age-old training in cunning and guile which has been instilled in the yellow races down through the early centuries of the world, when Occidentals were just emerging from a state of primitive barbarism.

This attendant was a perfect example of the point. Mentally, Wentworth compared his manners to those of any white doorman at any of the swanky night clubs in the city. The man's courtesy and speech were infinitely superior.

Wentworth nodded, smiling, matching the other's blandness. He glanced over the little man's shoulder, saw that the main dining room of the place had indeed undergone marvelous changes. Formerly, as he recalled it, the dining room had been a drab, smoky room, with the traditional dim lights and musty booths of the generally accepted Chinese restaurant.

But now it was something different. There were no booths. The room was decorated in the latest modernistic manner, with indirect lighting, octagonal tables, and the newest type of chairs, upholstered in rich leather upon tubular frames.

The floor of the restaurant itself was inlaid with tiles, and here was given the first hint of the Oriental background of the place; for the tiles were multicolored, arranged to represent figures and groups taken from old Chinese legends. Chinese waiters padded across the tiles, serving quietly and efficiently. In the center of the room a small dance floor was roped off, and at one end of the dance floor was a platform for the orchestra and the entertainers. At the moment, most of the couples were dancing.

Wentworth followed the attendant to a table near the wall, which was one of the few that were vacant. He had originally intended to ask for Nita van Sloan, and join her. But the developments of the evening had decided him against that course. If he were to be attacked again, he wanted to be alone when it happened; and in the event that Nita had not yet been spotted by the enemy, he did not want to draw attention to her.

He seated himself, and ordered a cocktail then allowed his eyes to stray over the room. There was the usual complement of out-of-towners at the various tables, staring in goggle-eyed amazement at the elaborate furnishings. Mow Loo Fen, the owner, must be a master of showmanship, Wentworth thought, to have conceived the idea of blending the extremely modernistic with the Oriental. In the cities of the Middle West, where many of these people came from, the "chop suey houses" were all of the same type and pattern, and if they had found the same here in New York they would not have been impressed. But this was different; they were willing to pay the exorbitant prices that Mow Loo Fen charged, because of that difference.

At a table close to the dance floor sat Nita van Sloan.

She had seen Wentworth enter, but when he did not approach her table she gave no sign of recognizing him. Quick-witted as she was, she immediately guessed that something had arisen to make it inadvisable to reveal the fact of their acquaintanceship. She was separated from him by three tables, but the distance was not too great for Wentworth to note that she was agitated about something. He threw her a significant glance, then looked around the place.

He at once spotted the two men whom he had seen entering just before. Nils Bishop and young Martin Custer were seated two tables down along the dance floor from where Nita sat. Martin Custer was leaning forward tensely, alternately drumming on the table top and toying with the stem of his cocktail glass. Nils Bishop was lolling back, completely at ease. There was a hint of a sardonic smile on the coarse features of the ex-international spy.

Wentworth could see that young Custer's eyes were fixed on some one or something across the dance floor, but it was impossible for him to tell what the young fellow was looking at, because of the press of dancers on the small dancing floor.

The music ceased, and the couples retired to their tables.

Wentworth glanced at Nita, and saw that she was flicking her fingernail against the edge of her empty cocktail glass. Each time her fingernail struck the glass, there would be a slight tinkle. Wentworth's eyes narrowed, and he suddenly tensed as he realized that those little tinkling sounds were not made haphazardly. They were long, short, long, spaced at definite intervals.

Nita was trying to send him a message by Morse Code!

FOR MANY weary hours on and off through the years, Wentworth had practiced tapping out Morse code, with Nita as well as with Jackson and Ram Singh; so that now, they were all proficient at sending and picking up messages from each other. They knew the Morse alphabet as well as their ABC's, and Wentworth had insisted that they become so expert that they could send and receive without the aid of paper and pencil.

He flashed her a quick glance, nodded almost imperceptibly to indicate that he was ready, and raised his cocktail glass to his lips, to cover his attentiveness to the message under the guise of taking a sip. He caught the code, translating the dots and dashes mentally:

D-o-n-t d-r-i-n-k... d-o-n-t d-r-i-n-k....

He had already taken a mouthful of the cocktail, but automatically, as the meaning of the message registered upon him, he reacted quickly to the warning. He held the liquid in his mouth, put the glass down.

The bar was at the back of the dining room, and he had been seated facing the front. Nita, on the other hand, was seated facing in the opposite direction, so that she could see what was taking place at the bar. She must have seen something that caused her to suspect the drink was doctored.

Slowly, with every appearance of casualness, he raised his napkin, appeared to wipe his mouth. In reality he spat the liquid into the cloth, then rolled the napkin carefully and replaced it in his lap. He was chagrined with himself at not having thought of the possibility of tampering with his drink. It was one more proof of the expertness of the organization of the Man from Singapore.

Nita went on playing with the glass, and the tinkling dots and dashes continued:

*Watch balcony other side dance floor...just saw doctor go there...
think man you wounded in that room....*

Nita ceased tapping on the glass just as the orchestra resumed
playing. Wentworth threw a glance up at the balcony. It ran the
entire length of the dining room, and there was doubtless some
other means of reaching it besides the spiral staircase which
he could see at the front. As he watched, he saw the door of
the office on the balcony open. A small man came out, carrying a doctor's bag. The man was thin, shriveled, with a slinking
appearance of furtiveness.

Wentworth knew him at once. He was Doctor Sunderson, who ran a down-at-heels compensation clinic nearby on
LaFayette Street. Sunderson's compensation work had fallen off
considerably in the past few years, due to the shady methods he
had used, and to the way he had padded his bills to the various
insurance companies and to the State Insurance Fund. But he
still maintained those offices, and his presence here was one
explanation of the way he was able to keep on making a living.

Sunderson started down the spiral staircase, after casting a
glance over the busy, gay dining room floor. And at that moment
the orchestra ceased playing for a moment. The short, sleek
Chinaman who had welcomed Wentworth at the door mounted
the platform, raised his hands for silence.

"And now, ladies and gentlemen," that worthy said, "we shall
be privileged to witness the dancing of the beautiful young lady
who has charmed our patrons in the past—Miss Laura Gay."

He bowed toward a table at the other side of the dance
floor, and all eyes were turned toward the dark-haired, almost

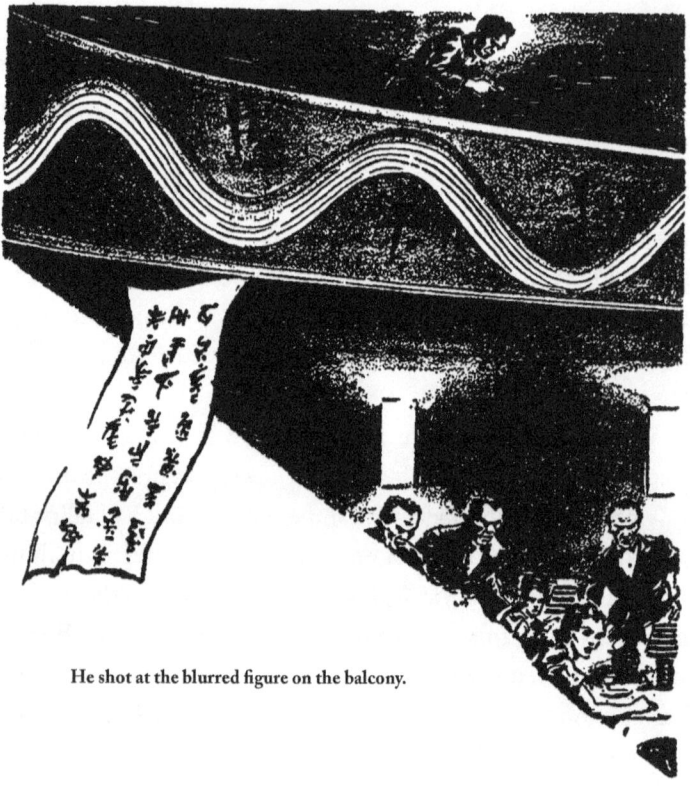

He shot at the blurred figure on the balcony.

regally beautiful young woman who sat there. Wentworth's eyes narrowed as he noted her companions at that table. There were three of them, *and they were all Chinese.*

Three bland, inscrutable Chinamen, sitting with one beautiful white woman in a public place—that in itself might not have been so startling, but for the fact that one of those Chinese, a stout, round-faced Oriental with a pockmarked skin, was lean-

ing close to her, whispering confidentially with one pudgy hand on the soft white roundness of her bare arm!

As the announcer spoke her name, Miss Laura Gay drew away from the round-faced Chinaman, and arose. She was dressed in a vivid scarlet evening gown that emphasized the contours of her svelte, slender form. Black hair was piled high on her head, and she carried herself with the grace and the litheness of a born dancer as she made her way through the aisles toward the platform, to the accompaniment of thunderous applause from the diners.

WENTWORTH'S ATTENTION was diverted from Doctor Sunderson, who had reached the main floor, and now was shifting in turn to Nita, young Martin Custer and his companion, Nils Bishop, and Laura Gay.

Suddenly he felt that an electric air of tension had entered the atmosphere. It was as if events were rapidly speeding toward a crisis of some sort. Laura Gay, though she carried herself lithely, gracefully, seemed straining under some great emotional burden. To the uninitiated she seemed merely a happy, carefree young dancer who was enjoying the plaudits of her public. Her smile seemed to be spontaneous, full of pleasant humor as she reached the platform and bowed to right and left.

But Wentworth saw her suddenly stiffen as her eyes met those of young Martin Custer, at the table near the edge of the dance floor. For a moment the smile faded from her lips, only to reappear there almost at once, as if forced back by a supreme effort of will.

Young Custer had half risen from his chair, both hands gripping hard at the edge of the table. He was looking up at the girl on the platform, with mouth half open as if to shout at her, and his chest was heaving with some pent-up emotion. Nils Bishop was watching him carefully, as a scientist might watch a rat upon which he was experimenting.

Laura Gay turned away from Custer, stepped back upon the platform, and the orchestra swung into the melody of a colorful Spanish dance. The orchestra leader stepped forward deferentially, to hand her a pair of castanets.

And abruptly young Custer uttered a hoarse shout, and pushed over his table. The two cocktail glasses fell to the floor, then the table followed with a crash. Custer sprang out on the dance floor, still uttering unintelligible shouts. He was as a man possessed. Nils Bishop did not follow him, but merely pushed his chair up, ignoring the overturned table, and got to his feet as if to afford himself a better view.

Laura Gay shrank away from young Custer, who leaped across the dance floor, and vaulted to the platform. The orchestra stopped playing and Custer's shouts became coherent, audible in the sudden silence.

"Laura!" he shouted. "Laura! Is it true? Have they got you?"

She retreated, sudden panic in her eyes, until her back was to the big bass drum. "No, no, Martin!" she virtually screamed. "Go away! You mustn't—"

"By God, I'll see!" he shouted. And reaching forth, he gripped the front of her dress, ripped it away with a savage jerk. This frail material tore down the front, revealing the soft white skin of

Laura Gay's body. Frantically she snatched at the hanging ends of the dress, tried to cover herself.

But it was too late. Everybody in the place had seen the ugly livid scar, in the shape of two horrible fangs, that disfigured her right breast!

The beautiful, talented Laura Gay carried the mark of the Man from Singapore!

Stunned silence pervaded the place—a silence that was torn asunder by the sudden loud, coarse laughter of Nils Bishop, who stood with his hands on his hips and laughed with loud, unsubdued enjoyment.

Young Custer stepped close to Laura Gay, who cowered in front of him. "You're marked!" he screamed. "Then it's true—true—true, everything is true! I loved you—and you're marked!"

Suddenly he raised his open hand, slapped her hard in the face.

Bishop's laughter still rang out loud and long. Two Chinese waiters were hurrying through the aisles toward the ex-spy, while four or five others were running across the dance floor toward the platform.

Wentworth half rose from his seat. Out of the corner of his eye he saw Doctor Sunderson sneaking around the edge of the room toward his table. He saw Nita sitting tensely looking toward him as if for a cue; and he also saw a blur of motion upon the balcony where the private office was located. One thing more he saw, and that was the small but compact group of Chinamen from the table which Laura Gay had left. Those three Chinamen did not seem concerned at all with the tableau on the platform. They were crossing the dance floor swiftly bearing down upon the table where Nita van Sloan sat. There was no mistaking their intention, for the eyes of all three were fixed upon her vindictively.

It almost seemed as if Custer's strange, impulsive, ill-considered action had been awaited as the signal for action.

All these things registered upon Wentworth's consciousness simultaneously in the split-second while Custer was striking Laura Gay. Now Custer swung around, glared across the floor at the boisterously laughing figure of Nils Bishop.

"Damn you!" Custer shouted, "I'll kill—"

That was as far as he got. There was a short, sharp report from the balcony and young Custer uttered a scream of pain, swayed and sank slowly to his knees. Blood spurted out from a wound just underneath his heart, staining his dinner jacket. His mouth opened to speak, but he suddenly fell to the floor of the platform, lay still.

WENTWORTH HAD arisen, pushed back his chair, and his hand snaked in and out from his shoulder holster, flicked up and fired almost in the same continuous motion. He shot at the blurred figure up there on the balcony whence had come the report of the gun that had shot Custer. He saw the figure jerk with the impact of his slug, then he swung around toward Nita's table. The three Chinamen were already upon her, and Nita had realized the danger, was fumbling in her purse for her own pistol. One of the three Chinamen reached out to grip her arm, and Wentworth, his lips clamped tightly together, shot the man in the shoulder, sent him spinning against the other two.

Nita sprang away from the table, her pistol out now, and Wentworth shouted to her: "Back entrance, Nita! Jackson's there!"

Almost before he finished, the lights suddenly went out all over the place. The entire dining room floor was plunged into darkness!

The echoes of the shots that had just been fired still rolled through the room, but they were drowned by the abrupt shrieks of panic and fear that came from the diners. They had been held spellbound for the moment by the swift kaleidoscopic action. Now, with the blackness of night blanketed around them, they gave way to panic. Shouts of men, screams of women, filled the darkness all around.

Wentworth started toward the spot where he had last seen Nita, and suddenly felt the impact of a body that lurched against him. His hand was seized in a bony grip, and a voice whispered: "Wentworth! For God's sake, get out quick!"

The lips that uttered that warning were close to his face, and he caught the smell of liquor and the odor of cigarettes.

"It's me—Sunderson!" the voice hurried on. "Come on—the back way! They weren't going to let me get out alive. Thank God for this chance—"

"Keep close to me!" Wentworth whispered. He pushed through struggling, shouting men and women, reached the table where Nita had been. He flicked on his fountain pen flashlight, saw that she was not there. The Chinaman he had wounded was lying on the dance floor, squirming in agony. But of the other two there was no sign.

Here and there, matches were flaring in the darkness, while from outside there came the squeal of a police whistle. Wentworth's flashlight made a luminous pencil of light, through which panicky figures ran. He frowned. Had Nita gotten out, or was she in the hands of the other two Chinese whom he had seen bearing down upon her?

Above the commotion in the room he heard the stentorian shouts of a police officer in the hall. His flashlight, sliding around over the room, picked up the huge figure of Nils Bishop, making toward the spiral staircase at the front of the room. Bishop was carrying a woman's figure over his shoulder. The woman was struggling and screaming and Wentworth threw the light in her face, saw that it was the dancer, Laura Gay.

He became conscious of sudden, slithery motion behind him, and whirled, swinging the flashlight. Its beam caught the gleam of glittering steel in the hand of Sunderson. The little doctor had opened his instrument bag, which was now lying on the floor at his feet, and had taken the keen-edged scalpel from it.

Sunderson recoiled as Wentworth swung his automatic to bear on him. "Don't worry, Wentworth!" he shouted. "I'll protect your back with this scalpel. Go ahead!"

Wentworth laughed shortly. "I'll go ahead all right—but not with you in back of me!"

He seized Sunderson by the collar, sent him lurching ahead with a shove. He did not know whether the doctor had sincerely meant to guard his back, or to stab him in the back. In the meantime, he was taking no chances.

The uniformed policemen were already in the room, using

their powerful flashlights. Had it not been for the disturbance down in the street, they would never have arrived so promptly. Wentworth had no desire to remain here and be questioned while he was still unaware of what had happened to Nita. Sunderson was running across the dance floor, and Wentworth's pencil beam kept track of him.

The doctor motioned to him to follow, and Wentworth pushed through the crowd, across the dining room, past the bar in the wake of Sunderson.

ABRUPTLY HE found himself in a hallway, and Sunderson whispered: "Come along. If we get down these stairs, we'll be in the alley at the rear."

They started down, the doctor in the lead. In a moment they were out in the narrow alley behind the building. The shouting upstairs had died down, and Wentworth could see that the lights had gone on again. Probably some one had found the switch.

In the street upon which the alley opened, they found Wentworth's limousine at the curb, with Jackson standing behind it, waiting anxiously.

"Have you seen Miss van Sloan?" Wentworth demanded.

Jackson shook his head. "No sir. You're the first to come out of that alley. You—you think something happened to her, sir?"

Wentworth's eyes were bleak. "I'm afraid the Man from Singapore has her," he said grimly.

Doctor Sunderson exclaimed: "That girl—the one the Chinese were rushing at, and whom you called out to. Is she the one you are worried about?"

Wentworth nodded. "What about her?"

"She went out the same way we did, just ahead of us. I saw her running, with the Chinese behind her."

Wentworth studied Sunderson's face. "Then she must have come out of this alley—"

"Impossible, sir," Jackson interrupted. "I was here every moment. No one came out."

Sunderson laughed. "There are at least two other ways out of that alley that I know of—and there may be more. The Chinese probably caught her on the staircase or in the alley, and took her away."

Sunderson was holding the scalpel in his right fist, with the blade down, like a poniard. Suddenly he uttered a scream, and pointed toward the alley. Several slinking shapes were coming out from the darkness there, and metal glinted in yellow hands.

Sunderson shouted: "Don't let them get me! Save me!"

He raised his knife, flung it at the dark shapes, and then started to run, his knees wobbling, down the street. Wentworth and Jackson both had their guns out now, but those dark figures did not attack. Instead, they retreated back into the alley, silently, as if they had been ghosts.

Wentworth frowned, started after them, but Jackson plucked at his sleeve. "We better not stay, sir. There's a police siren around the corner. They'll have the block surrounded in no time, now. You'll most certainly be held for questioning, since you were seen shooting in there."

"You're right, Jackson," Wentworth said shortly. He swung around to look for the doctor. "Hello! Where's Sunderson?"

Doctor Sunderson had disappeared!

Jackson plucked at his sleeve. "Let's go, sir. We've no time—"

"And leave without knowing what's happened to Nita?"

"We can come back, sir. If she's in there, the police will find her. Otherwise, I'm thinking it will be a job for—the Spider!"

Wentworth's eyes gleamed. "Are my hat and cloak in the car?"

"Yes, sir."

"Let's go, then. Drive a couple of blocks away, then stop."

As the limousine pulled away from the curb, the first of the bluecoats came out of the alley. Apparently they had not encountered the Chinese who had been there only a few moments ago. The limousine was already at the far corner. Wentworth, looking out through the rear window, said bleakly: "Round One goes to you Mr. Man from Singapore, I think." His eyes had the hardness of flint. "But we'll be back for Round Two—I promise it!"

CHAPTER 4
AHMED KUPRA-SING

IT WAS a large room, as rooms go in Chinatown. The sole illumination was furnished by the dancing flames of a huge brazier in the center of the floor, thus leaving the four corners in comparative darkness.

The room was perhaps twenty feet in length, and the same distance across. There was a narrow door in the exact center of each of the four walls. The walls themselves were covered by woven tapestries of a deep maroon color, embellished with figures of Buddhas and dragons, similar to the figures inlaid upon the tiled floor of the Eating Place of Mow Loo Fen.

The only openings in the hangings were at the doors, where the expensive drapes were tied back by cords that resembled the braided hair of a woman. In front of each of the doors stood a tall, raw-boned coolie, naked except for a loin cloth. The heads of the coolies were closely shaven, making them appear even more ugly and brutish. Each coolie stood stiffly erect, with a long, wicked curved sabre in his right hand. The silence in the room was deep, utter.

Nita van Sloan was standing before the hot brazier.

She was still clad in the evening gown which she had worn at the Eating Place of Mow Loo Fen, but the dress was torn in several places, and there were two long scratches on her right cheek—mute evidence of the struggle she had put up.

Her hands were tied behind her back, with the wrists dragged up high against her shoulder blades. A cord, cunningly devised, ran from the bonds upon her wrists in a loop up around her neck, so that if she should try to lower her hands behind her, the loop would strangle her. The cords were made of toughened catgut, which would not give or stretch. Another length of catgut bound her ankles together. In this position it was impossible for her to bend forward by so much as an inch without straining the cord against her throat.

On either side of her stood two more coolies, also naked save for their loin cloths, and armed, like those at the doors, with long sabres. Nita's eyes were both defiant and expectant. They strayed from one wall to the other, surveying the figures woven upon the tapestry coverings. She was less than two feet from the brazier, and the hot flames licked upward, throwing her face into sharp relief, tingeing her cheeks with a ruddy glow. The heat in the room was almost unbearable, and she could see the sweat pouring down the naked torsos of the coolies; yet they made no move to wipe away the perspiration, but stood stoically unmoving.

Suddenly, the muted peals of a deep-toned gong sounded somewhere, not far off. The four guards, as well as Nita's two captors, stiffened, and raised their sabres to salute. They remained motionless thus, for perhaps two minutes. Then, the door in the wall which Nita was facing was thrown open, and a short, squat Chinaman entered. He was dressed in conventional Western garb. He was one of the three who had rushed at Nita across the dance floor, just before the lights were turned out.

This man paused a moment, sweeping the room with an all-embracing glance, then said unctuously: "So solly to double you like this, Miss van Sloan. The Man from Singapore will see you now." The peculiar twist of his lips belied the silken softness of his words.

Nita did not answer, but kept her eyes fixed upon the door. The Chinaman who had just entered turned toward the door and bowed low. "He comes. The Man from Singapore!"

A strange tenseness suddenly pervaded the room. Heavy footfalls sounded outside, and then—the Man from Singapore appeared in the doorway!

Nita uttered a gasp of amazement and revulsion.

THE MAN from Singapore was sitting in a wheel chair, which was being pushed by another of the half naked coolies. The lower part of his body was covered by a heavy robe, so that his legs were invisible, if he had any. He wore a red silk jacket with wide, capacious sleeves into which his hands were thrust. About his neck there hung a queer, revolting necklace that seemed to be made of the fangs of some wild beast.

But Nita saw little of all this. Her eyes were riveted in utter fascination upon the face of the Man from Singapore.

That face was coal black. A low forehead tapered backward to a shock of thick black hair that stood up straight like the bristles of a brush. The Man's face was full, almost stout; with high cheekbones and a flat, wide nose, a broad red slash of a mouth that was open to reveal long, almost fang-like teeth—the whole head set upon a wide, stubby trunk of a neck; eyes small, deepsunken and set close together; eyes that peered out at Nita with a feverish, vivid sort of bestial curiosity—such was the Man from Singapore!

Nita barely restrained a shudder, forced herself to a cool, summarizing scrutiny of this atrocity in the shape of a human being. Whether this man was a cripple or not, she could not tell. As to his race, she was equally in the dark. Negroid, Malayan, Chinese—or a mixture of all three? She felt a queer sense of unreality, of helplessness, as she met the gaze of the man in the wheel chair. Her body felt suddenly cold. She seemed to feel that there, in that wheel chair, sat the epitome of all that was vicious and evil.

The Man from Singapore! How aptly, she thought, had he named himself. From what other part of the world could such a being come, than from Singapore—where twin-screw modern liners from the West scraped paint at the crowded docks with Chinese junks, Malay sampans, and tramp steamers from every port in the East; from Singapore, where every color, creed and caste is found swarming in the streets; where burnoosed Arabs rub shoulders with shuffling Chinamen, with natives from Malaysia, with swart Tibetans from Lhassa, and with shifty-eyed, sickly Eurasians many of whom could not even name their homeland? Only a city like Singapore, Nita thought, could have bred a monstrosity like this—a mixture of negroid, Chinese, Malayan, and the Devil-knew-what in one man!

LAURA GAY

JOHN CUSTER

NILS BISHOP

THE MAN
FROM
SINGAPORE

THE OLD
FLOWER WOMAN

No one spoke a word while the coolie attendant wheeled the chair to the left, and swung it behind a teakwood desk.

The flames from the brazier were intensely hot, but they left the far ends of the room in dimness, so that the face of the man in the chair seemed to Nita to be swimming in a mist of sliminess. She watched him breathlessly as he settled himself behind the teakwood desk, with the stout Chinese standing obsequiously behind him.

He said curtly to this one, in sharp, clipped English: "Announce me, Mow Loo Fen!"

Nita started. So this stout Chinaman was Mow Loo Fen, the owner of the restaurant where she had been seized! She remembered vividly the few moments that followed the shooting, when the lights went out.

Wentworth had shouted to her to make for the rear exit, and she had started in that direction, feeling her way at the edge of the dance floor. But she had taken only two steps before she felt the soft, slimy bodies of those Chinamen upon her. She had tried to use her small pistol, but her hand had been seized, twisted. At the same time, some one clamped a wet cloth of chloroform upon her nose.

She had fought desperately against it, had kicked out viciously with her heels, bringing a howl of pain, and had succeeded in breaking away from her captors. She ran, staggering, dizzy and nauseous toward the rear, and found the exit, which she had been careful to spot soon after entering. She knew, even as she went through that rear door, that she had not shaken off her Chinese attackers, even in the darkness.

And sure enough, they had caught up with her on the stairs. She turned and fought bitterly, clawing with her fingernails and beating at them with her fists. But it was no use. Once more, inexorably, that cloth soaked in chloroform was pressed against her nostrils, and this time she could not resist. She lost consciousness.

When she awoke, she found herself in a room adjoining this one, lying on the floor, trussed up as she was now. And then they had brought her in here.

Whether she was still in the building of the restaurant, or whether she had been taken to another place miles away, she did not know. But she had learned, at least, that the restaurant proprietor, Mow Loo Fen, was a servant of the Man from Singapore.

SHE WATCHED breathlessly while Mow Loo Fen bowed low, then straightened up and intoned in a sing-song voice, looking directly at Nita: "Woman of the white barbarians, bow low your head; for you have the honor and the privilege to stand in the presence of the Highest of All the High, The Man from Singapore—Ahmed Kupra-sing, the Emperor of all the Oriental Races in the Western Hemisphere!"

Nita's lips pursed, and swift thoughts flashed through her mind. This then, was the answer to the campaign of terror and murder that was spreading over Chinatown!

"The Emperor of all the Oriental Races in the Western Hemisphere!"

The name of Ahmed Kupra-sing meant nothing to her; but the title which Mow Loo Fen had placed after the name of the Man from Singapore spoke volumes to Nita. Many men from the eastern portion of the globe had aspired, in the past, to the role of dictator of the yellow races in the West. Dreams of power and glory had been built upon the idea of being the absolute lord of all the Chinese who dwelt in America. Thus far, such dreams had been impossible of realization because of the various tongs that already existed, demanding the allegiance of large groups of Chinese. But here was a man who was actually waging a campaign to bring all the Oriental races under his influence! If he should succeed, he might prove a greater menace to the safety of the country than had ever been faced in our history!

Nita studied the revolting face of Ahmed Kupra-sing once more, with renewed interest. The Man from Singapore sat in the shadow, and there was little that she could see beyond what she had already seen of him.

Mow Loo Fen repeated sternly: "Bow your head, woman!"

Nita forced a smile. The cords were straining against her throat now, and the agony of holding her wrists high behind her back was becoming greater and greater.

"Even the Highest of All the High," she said ironically, "cannot demand the impossible. These cords weren't arranged for head-bowing."

The two coolies who stood guard over her seized her roughly by the arms, as if to chastise her for speaking so disrespectfully to their master. Mow Loo Fen frowned at her.

But Ahmed Kupra-sing withdrew a black hand from one of his sleeves, raised it. The coolies stepped back, releasing their hold upon Nita.

"I will talk with her," he said. His voice was harsh, grating. But his words were clearly and distinctly enunciated. Nita judged that it was the enunciation of a foreigner who has learned English in a good school, one who had been well educated. She wondered fleetingly where a man like this could have acquired a good education.

And then Ahmed Kupra-sing was saying: "You do not fear me? You do not fear the Man from Singapore? Men have died with my name upon their lips. I am one to be feared."

Nita stood erect, her lips firm, her eyes fixed clearly upon the man in the wheel chair, smiling defiantly in spite of the agony in her arms.

"I am very much afraid," she said evenly: "It is no disgrace to be afraid. But what good is it to show fear before a beast? It only infuriates him the more!"

Mow Loo Fen took an angry step forward, and the coolies on guard at the doors, who apparently understood a little English, raised their sabres.

But Ahmed laughed. His hideous face broke into a queer, revolting travesty of a grin. "They say in the East that 'it is a brave man who fears not to show his fear.' I am thinking that you are a brave woman." He paused, then went on; and his voice assumed a strange, forbidding resonance. "But perhaps you do not really understand what fear is. Perhaps you do not understand my power."

"Is it necessary?" Nita asked contemptuously.

"It is necessary. You are a person whom I wish to convince—for reasons which I shall tell you later." He raised his voice, issued a series of swift orders in a language that Nita did not understand but which she took to be Cantonese.

At once her two coolie guards stepped forward, and one of them raised his sabre. Nita steeled herself for the blow that was to come, but the coolie did not strike her. Instead, he slashed with the edge of his sabre at the catgut cord looped around her neck, then cut once more at the cord binding her wrists.

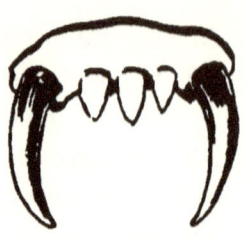

She was free!

FOR A moment she stared unbeliev-ingly at the Man from Singapore. He laughed harshly. "I wish your hands to be free—when you see what I have to show you!"

Nita's arms tingled as the blood flowed down into them. She felt gingerly of her throat where the cord had left a line of red, tender skin.

Ahmed's voice changed, became softly purring. "You," he said, "are Miss Nita van Sloan. You are the friend and fiancée of Richard Wentworth—*the man who is known as the Spider!*"

Nita suddenly felt herself trembling, cold and shaky. This was a greater disaster than she had anticipated. For herself to be a prisoner of the Man from Singapore before the battle had well begun, was bad enough. But now she realized that Ahmed Kupra-sing held all the cards; he knew who the Spider was, knew that Richard Wentworth was his enemy. And Wentworth did not know who he was.

Nita remained silent, waiting for him to go on.

Ahmed chuckled wickedly. "Charlie Wing was deliberately goaded on, to the point where he appealed to the Spider. You see, I knew that the Spider had helped him once before, and if he were in trouble, he would go to him again. In that way, I was able to learn who the Spider is."

Nita's eyes narrowed. She tried to think back swiftly over the last few hours, and she realized that Wentworth had not really said anything to indicate that Charlie Wing had phoned to the apartment. She realized now that Charlie must have phoned to Laskar, Wentworth had kept that information from her.

"Why did you do all this?" she asked levelly, forcing herself to hide the revulsion in her eyes at sight of that hideous black face of the Man from Singapore.

"Because, my dear young lady, I wanted to spike the Spider's guns before he started. Within a few days, the name of the Man from Singapore will be on the lips of everybody in the two Americas. I will be well on the way to realizing my ambition—an ambition that I have nursed for many years."

Ahmed Kupra-sing leaned forward, and his voice assumed a new tone of fanatical intensity. "In a few days I shall be hailed throughout America as the Highest of All the High, the Emperor of all the Oriental Races in the Western Hemisphere. Do you think, Miss van Sloan, that I did not plan carefully and well for this coup? I knew that the Spider would inevitably be attracted into the case—and I arranged to eliminate him before he became dangerous!"

Nita asked breathlessly: "You—have eliminated him?"

"Not yet, I regret to say. So far, he has proved too clever, too good a fighter. He has already walked through three distinct traps. But he cannot fail to yield!"

"What—what do you mean?"

"I mean you, dear young lady. The Spider has always been a formidable opponent. But he has a weakness—an Achilles' Heel.

That weakness is you. He will not fight me if he knows that it will cost him your life!"

Nita laughed scornfully. "You don't know the Spider! If you are planning to hold me as a hostage, you will be disappointed." Boldly she lied, hoping to make the he sound effective. "My life means no more to the Spider than his own; and he risks his life continually. No threat to me would stop him—"

"Perhaps not an ordinary threat, dear lady. But I am sure he will not want to see your beautiful young body treated—like this!"

Abruptly, the Man from Singapore clapped his hands twice in quick succession. The coolie at the door to the left of Nita bowed low, then straightened and put his hand on a lever alongside the door. He stood, gripping the lever, and looking toward Ahmed, who clapped his hands once more. The coolie pulled the lever all the way down, and the door, instead of opening inward, began to slide apart, in two halves. Nita gasped as she realized that not only the door, but the whole wall, on that side of the room, was sliding open.

The walls slid open to a width of about ten feet, revealing a small chamber, the contents of which caused Nita to catch her breath in sudden dismay.

In the center of this chamber there stood a weird contraption of metal. It was perhaps six feet long, and it rested on thick legs of iron. Its top consisted of a slab of metal, studded in the center with spikes which protruded to a height of about four inches.

And on her back on those spikes lay the naked body of the dancer, Laura Gay.

CHAPTER 5
BRIDE OF THE SPIKED HORSE

HER SHOULDERS and ankles rested upon ridges of the metal horse, so that by arching her back she could keep her body from pressing against the points of the spikes. Her wrists and ankles were shackled to the iron horse, and the unfortunate girl twisted her face toward where Nita stood, her eyes carrying a message of misery and appeal.

Nita stared, wide-eyed with horror. Directly above the body of Laura Gay an oblong slab of metal hung suspended by a system of pulleys, which were operated by a lever in a corner of the small chamber. At this lever stood another Chinese, who was watching the shackled dancer.

The slab of metal was thick, and appeared to be very heavy. It was some four feet long, and as wide as the iron horse above which it hung. Nita shivered as she realized the purpose of that slab.

By moving the lever, the Chinese could lower it so that it rested upon the body of Laura Gay, pressing her down upon the spikes. When the full weight of that slab finally rested upon the prisoner, it would force her body down so that the spikes would pierce her back, gradually wedge in, deeper and deeper. She would be conscious for hours while those spikes were torturing her vitals.

A sardonic cackling laugh from Ahmed Kupra-sing caused Nita to whirl around. The Man from Singapore was watching

73

the efforts of the dancer to keep her body off the spikes. And he was laughing with fiendish amusement.

"You see, Miss van Sloan, how ingenious my assistants are? This young lady has some information which I am anxious to get. This is one of my methods for—er—inducing reluctant persons to talk!"

The black face of the Man from Singapore, half obscured by the shadows in the corner where he sat, seemed to be the face of some obscene creature of the night. He turned toward the chamber of torture, and spoke to the prisoner, his voice assuming a quality of steely ruthlessness.

"Miss Gay, you have a last chance to speak, before that beautiful body of yours is mutilated. I want to know the name of the big, fair-haired man who accompanied young Martin Custer to the Eating Place of Mow Loo Fen tonight. It was he who guided him, apparently he who told him that you bore my mark. In the darkness, he escaped. *I want to know who he is!*"

Laura Gay, apparently exhausted from the dreadful effort of keeping her back constantly arched, allowed her body to sag for an instant. The sharp points of the spikes dug at her skin, and she groaned, raised herself frantically.

"God, take me off! I tell you, I don't know who he is. I never saw him before—"

"You know, and you will speak!" Ahmed's voice thundered. He addressed the man at the lever. "Proceed, Sin Took. Give her a little dose of the spiked horse. When she is ready to talk, notify me!"

Sin Took grinned, bowed, and pulled the lever over a little.

The heavy metal slab began to descend inexorably toward the white, glistening body of Laura Gay.

The dancer screamed, writhed in her shackles. There was no way of avoiding the descending slab.

"For God's sake, let me go!" she shrieked. "I swear to God I don't know who that man was! In the name of God—"

Her voice was cut short by the walls of the room, which swiftly slid back into place, shutting out from Nita's eyes the scene of torture. Nita had stood there, trembling with sympathy for the poor dancer. In another instant, she might have yielded to impulse, and rushed forward, without a thought of the odds against her. But Ahmed Kupra-sing must have read her mind. He had signaled with his hand, and the walls closed before her.

Nita swung toward the Man from Singapore. "You devil!" she exclaimed.

Ahmed laughed. "I showed you that so you would understand what pressure I could bring upon you, my dear young lady. In this place there is no room for mercy or softness. We have a great ambition, and no person or thing shall be allowed to stand in the way of that ambition-no, not even the Spider!"

THE SIGHT of that dreadful torture machine in the next chamber still swam before Nita's eyes. She could still see the agonized, terror-stricken face of the shackled Laura Gay, could even imagine the tortured girl in there now, shrieking out her heart in the unbearable agony of those spikes.

Desperately, Nita looked for some way out. She was not counting consequences now; she was thinking only of some way to save the dancer. Her eyes fell on the two coolies who

Her flashing blade was everywhere. Yet they were five....

were guarding her, with bare sabres. There were four more of them in the room, in addition to Mow Loo Fen and the Man from Singapore. If she could only get possession of one of those sabres, hold its point at the heart of the Man from Singapore, trade his life for the life of Laura Gay! Or perhaps she could run him through, rid society of this new menace that was weaving a net of intrigue and murder among the yellow races!

Nita van Sloan, from long association with Richard Wentworth, had learned to act swiftly once a decision was made. Even while the Man from Singapore was still talking, she took a quick step to the left, brought her open left hand around in a stiff blow to the side of the coolie's neck. She struck with the edge of her hand, putting all her strength into the effort.

It was a blow Wentworth had taught her, one which, if it strikes the right place, will paralyze a man's whole nervous system, cause him to collapse instantly. In order to be successful, the blow must hit a spot approximately an inch below the base of the ear, and three-quarters of an inch behind it. A slight deviation would cause it to be of little value or no effect. She had practiced it on a dummy in Wentworth's gym, hundreds of times, but she had never tried it on a living man with the force she was now using.

Her heart raced as the edge of her hand landed on the coolie's neck. Everything depended upon the accuracy with which the blow was placed. She would not have a chance to repeat it.

And it was successful. The coolie reeled, uttered a deep sigh, and suddenly pitched forward as if he had been propelled by a mighty battering ram in the small of his back. The sabre fell from his nerveless fingers, dropped soundlessly upon the deeply carpeted floor.

Almost before it reached the ground, and before the other coolies or the Man from Singapore realized what was happening, Nita bent and snatched up the sabre, leaped over the prostrate body of the coolie, directly toward the wheel chair of Ahmed Kupra-sing.

The black-faced Man from Singapore uttered a shrieking curse of terror and hate, and half rose in his chair, supporting himself by his arms. Mow Loo Fen stood frozen, dazed by the swift action. None of the coolies was near enough to intercept her. Fierce triumph welled in Nita's breast at the prospect of success.

And in that instant disaster came.

The outstretched arm of the coolie she had felled lay directly in her path, and the high heel of her evening slipper caught in the contorted yellow fingers. She tripped, fell headlong forward, and sprawled on the floor.

The coolies uttered shouts of wicked glee, and leaped toward her, raising their sabres. Ahmed Kupra-sing screamed to them in Cantonese, ordering them to seize her.

The nearest of the coolies reached her, bent to grip her hair, while the others closed in.

Nita squirmed away from the man, twisted to her knees, and brought her sabre up in a flat backhanded blow that caught the coolie across the face, sent him staggering backward.

Nita jumped to her feet just as the other coolies came at her, with sabres flashing. She backed away from them, her own weapon describing swift, sure arcs that kept her attackers at bay. She was no stranger to the weapon. Almost daily she and Ram Singh and Jackson and Wentworth took turns with the foils, keeping fit and trim.

From Wentworth she had learned tricks of fencing which made her the superior of all but expert swordsmen. She could handle a blade with deadly skill, and she fought desperately now, putting to use every ounce of her strength, every scintilla of skill that she had acquired.

The five coolies who attacked her, forming a short semicircle in front of her, were far from expert swordsmen. Her flashing blade was everywhere, engaging theirs, lunging and parrying with almost eye-defying swiftness. Yet they were five, and she was only one.

From his wheel chair the Man from Singapore shouted frantic encouragement to his men, while Mow Loo Fen danced about wildly.

Nita fought in silence, conserving her energy. Sparks flew as blade engaged blade, and the air was filled with the quick deadly tinkle of steel against steel.

THE SEMICIRCLE was slowly closing in, pushing her back toward the far wall, away from the flaming brazier, toward the shadow. Nita seized an opportunity to lunge, and the point of her sabre grated against bone as she ran a coolie through the chest. The man screamed, fell away, leaving only four attackers.

But in the instant that it took her to disengage her blade from the man's body, four other blades flicked in at her. One reached

NITA VAN SLOAN

its mark, gashed her shoulder, ripping the dress and cutting a bloody furrow in her white skin.

Nita hardly felt the wound. She retreated, trying to get her back to the wall so as to forestall the circumventing movement of the remaining attackers. Once they got in behind her, she would have no chance at all.

She called upon all her excess reserves of strength, kept her sabre moving in the air like a live thing, holding the coolies at their distance. From the far corner, on the other side of the brazier, came Ahmed Kupra-sing's voice, shrieking shrill instructions to his men in Cantonese.

Nita suddenly felt her back against the wall. Now she fought with greater assurance, with more purpose. Once again her blade licked out, this time catching one of the coolies in the throat. The coolie gurgled, dropped his sword, and flailed out with both hands in the agony of his wound. Then blood spurted from his lips, nose and from the wound in his throat. He thrashed about wildly for a moment, and his fellows crowded out of his way. Then he suddenly ceased thrashing and quietly collapsed to the floor in a tumbled heap.

That instant of diversion, while the coolies were getting out of the way of their wounded companion, gave Nita her opportunity. She slid a few feet to the left along the wall, then darted across the room toward the far corner where Ahmed sat.

The coolies shouted, came after her. Mow Loo Fen, standing beside Ahmed's chair, reached frantically into his pocket and dragged out a pistol. Why he had not produced it before, Nita

had no way of knowing; perhaps because he could not have used it accurately while the coolies were crowding about her. But now it constituted a serious threat.

Mow Loo Fen raised the pistol, aimed it carefully at Nita. Nita was just approaching the center of the room where the brazier burned when she saw Mow Loo Fen's gun, realized that she could never reach the chair of the Man from Singapore.

Almost without thinking, she swerved to one side, taking shelter from the pistol behind the brazier. The coolies were almost upon her once more. Now she would have to fight them, while Mow Loo Fen would be free to steal up behind her and shoot her in the back.

Nita smiled tightly as she fended off the thirsty sabres of the coolies. With her right hand she reached out, seized the handle of the brazier, and yanked at it mightily!

The brazier and the stand tipped toward her, and she pulled harder, till she felt that the center of gravity of the brazier was far enough out to cause it to fall. Then she stepped nimbly to one side, letting go the handle.

The brazier went over with a crash, spilling its contents of perfumed wood and live coals upon the thick-napped rug. Almost at once flames sprung up from the rug, licking into the air.

The coolies began to shout, and leaped to put out the fire, beating at it with the flat of then blades. Ahmed Kupra-sing yelled at them, and they abandoned their frantic fire-fighting and turned after Nita. But she was already across the room, pressing at the lever which she had seen the coolie guard press to cause the walls to slide back. At once the hangings began to part as the walls went into motion.

Mow Loo Fen raised his pistol again, his almond eyes gleaming with triumph, for he had a perfect shot at Nita. But at that moment the shouting coolies bore down upon her, coming directly within the line of fire. Mow Loo Fen uttered a high-pitched curse, and ran forward to get a better shot.

BUT THE walls were open now, wide enough for Nita to pass through. She slipped through the opening, saw the figure of the Chinese executioner bearing down upon her with an immense crowbar.

Without hesitation she ran him through the heart, swung back and sent her sabre point licking through the opening in the walls to keep back the pursuing coolies.

They leaped back from her flashing blade, and Nita reached out, touched the button on the inner side of the door, which she saw in the framework. Apparently the walls could be operated from both sides, for the opening ceased to widen, began to close up again.

Narrower, narrower it became, until there was only an inch to go. And all the time Nita's blade was darting in and out through that ever narrowing space, keeping the coolies back from the doorway, away from the button on their side which would cause the walls to slide open again.

She could see Mow Loo Fen dancing about behind the coolies, shouting to them to get out of the way so he could get in a single shot; she could also see the flames from the over-turned brazier leaping up from the rug, could see them spreading swiftly toward the walls, to transform that big room into a roaring furnace.

And suddenly, the two sliding walls met. There was no longer an opening!

Nita swung away, picked up the crowbar which the Chinese executioner had dropped, and swung it in a smashing blow against the door lintel, just above the spot where the button was located. The crowbar landed with a splintering crash, leaving a deep dent in the wood of the lintel, and sending a tingling sensation up Nita's arms. But she smiled wearily. She had accomplished her purpose. The switch controlling those sliding walls was smashed. The men in the next room would have to seek some other means of getting at her.

Nita turned toward the spiked horse in the center of the room.

"You poor kid!" she exclaimed.

Laura Gay was lying with her back touching the points of the spikes, the huge, heavy metal slab resting upon her body. It had apparently just been brought this far down when Nita broke in.

Laura Gay's lips were white with agony, and her eyes were wet with tears. "Quick!" she begged. "I—I can't stand—this— any longer!"

"In a minute!" Nita told her, and ran across the room, seized the lever. Luckily she recalled the direction in which the executioner had pulled it, and she pushed it in the opposite direction. The metal slab responded, began to rise on its pulleys. In a moment it was off Laura Gay's body, and far enough up to allow clearance.

Nita left the lever, stepped swiftly to the body of the dead executioner, and went through his pockets, trying to avoid getting blood on her hands. She was looking for keys. She had seen that the shackles which bound the dancer to the spiked horse consisted of individual sets of handcuffs, one pair for each ankle and for each wrist.

While she searched the dead man's pockets, she could hear no sound from the other side of the wall. She recalled that when she had been in the other room, the closing walls had drowned out Laura Gay's screams, and she concluded that the walls must be soundproof. She hoped that Mow Loo Fen and Ahmed and their coolies were being kept busy putting out the fire. Otherwise, they would be here before she could get the girl free. Even now they might be hurrying around by some passage, to come at the room through the door in the far wall.

Frantically she went through one pocket after another of the dead executioner's clothes, mastering her revulsion at handling the bloody body. At last she raised her eyes, looking hopelessly at the shackled dancer.

"The keys!" she exclaimed. "I—I can't find them!"

Laura Gay moaned: "He had them before—"

It was becoming hot near the wall, where Nita knelt. The flames in the next room must be spreading. At any moment those coolies might enter.

Suddenly Nita's eyes flashed. She had been looking desperately about the chamber, and she caught the glitter of metal over against the far wall, near the lever. She ran across, stooped and snatched up the key ring which was lying there. A dozen keys were attached to that ring, but Nita at once picked the small handcuff key.

FRANTICALLY SHE worked at the shackles on Laura Gay's ankles and wrists. The single key fitted all the locks. One after another they dropped to the floor as Nita opened them. Then she aided the dancer to rise slowly off the spiked horse.

Laura Gay moaned with pain as she eased her body off the spikes. Her back, from shoulders to hips, was studded with small red spots from which blood was already welling. She could barely stand when she got to her feet, and Nita had to support her, at the same time looking around for something to cover her nakedness with.

"My—clothes!" gasped Laura Gay, motioning feebly to a small pile of things on a table in a corner.

Nita snatched up the dancer's evening gown. "Never mind the underthings. Slip that on quickly!"

She aided the girl to get her dress on, then helped her across the room. The small door in the far wall was unlocked, and they stepped through, found themselves on a landing, with a flight of stairs leading up, and another leading down. A hallway ran along the wall of the room they had just left, and Nita could see four or five other doors along that hall. From one of those doors, which was open, came clouds of billowing smoke and flame.

That was the room where she had left Ahmed Kupra-sing. Men were shouting in there, and as she watched she saw his wheel chair come rolling out through the flames, propelled by Mow Loo Fen.

After the wheel chair came the coolies, running with their

arms thrown across their faces to protect themselves from the fire. Nita understood now why they had not come sooner to intercept them. The fire must have spread so quickly that they were caught in the room. Mow Loo Fen's clothing was burning in two places, and the coolies helped to beat out the flames.

The Man from Singapore saw Nita and Laura Gay, and uttered a shout. The coolies swung around, and started to run toward the landing where they stood. Two of them had sabres, the others having probably lost their weapons in the fire.

Nita did not stay to fight them now. She could see flames pouring out from the room of the brazier. Soon this whole place would be a roaring inferno.

Throwing her arm around Laura Gay's waist, she hurried her down the stairs, with the coolies coming closely behind them, the two with the sabres in the lead.

At the foot of the stairs, the two girls stopped, amazed. Nita had had no idea where this place was located. Now she knew.

The foot of the stairs where they stood was a wooden landing, projecting some five feet out, and black, swirling water lapped at the beams. This house was certainly not in the building of the Eating Place of Mow Loo Fen. It was at the waterfront somewhere, whether the Hudson or the East River, she could not tell.

The coolies were coming down fast, and Laura Gay cowered in Nita's arms.

"T—they've got us!" she stammered.

"Not yet!" Nita said resolutely. "Can you swim?"

The girl nodded.

"Come on then—jump!"

She pushed Laura Gay to the edge of the landing, shoved her over, and dived after her just as the first of the coolies leaped down upon the landing. Laura Gay floundered in the water a moment, and Nita came to her aid, then the two girls swam off and were swallowed by the night, while the helpless coolies, unable to swim, danced frantically on the landing.

Fire rumbled within the building, and tongues of flame began to lick out from the windows. Somewhere, the clang of fire engines sounded....

CHAPTER 6
TWIN OF TROUBLE

RICHARD WENTWORTH stood tensely watching the line-up of sullen Chinamen who were being questioned by the police. These were the men who had been taken into custody at the Eating Place of Mow Loo Fen.

For hours on end they had been subjected to intensive interrogation, but no bit of information could be gleaned from them. They stubbornly persisted in their claim that they were merely employed at Mow Loo Fen's as waiters, cooks or bus boys, and that they knew nothing of any Man from Singapore, or of anything else, for that matter.

Finally, Commissioner Kirkpatrick, who was personally conducting the investigation, turned away from the last yellow man. Kirkpatrick was chewing nervously at a cigar as he approached Wentworth.

"It's no good, Dick! Not a word will they say. They claim they didn't even see young Custer shot! And we couldn't find a thing at the restaurant. We literally took Mow Loo Fen's place apart, but there isn't a shred of a clue, no trace of Nita. Have you tried your apartment again? Maybe she got away at that. Perhaps she's called—"

"I've been phoning Ram Singh at the apartment, every half hour all through the night," Wentworth told him bitterly. "There's no word from Nita. I should have gone back in there instead of leaving."

"It looks as if she's in the hands of the Man from Singapore, all right," Kirkpatrick said. "And that dancer, Laura Gay—she's missing too, together with your friend, Nils Bishop. I wonder what his purpose was in taking young Custer there? It almost looks as if he *wanted* the young chap to start something and get himself killed!"

The two men walked toward the door. "There's nothing more we can do here, Dick," the commissioner went on. "All of China-town is in turmoil, and I've got patrols out in every street. The Chinese are jittery, and something may break any minute that will give us a clue to work on. I've broadcast descriptions of both Nils Bishop and of Doctor Sunderson, and they ought to be picked up shortly. So why don't you go home and get some sleep?"

"Sleep!" Wentworth exclaimed bitterly. "Do you think I could sleep while Nita is in the hands of the Man from Singapore? I'm going back to Mow Loo Fen's. Maybe I can pick up something that was overlooked by your men."

He was about to leave, when one of the plain clothes men in

the room approached Kirkpatrick, saluted and reported: "There's a report of a fire down by the East River, sir. It's not far from Chinatown, and I thought you ought to know about it."

Kirkpatrick waved his hand impatiently. "Thanks, Grady, but I've got other things to think about. Handle it yourself—"

"Wait!" Wentworth interrupted. "We've got so little to go on, we can't afford to overlook a single thing. Let's hear the report."

Kirkpatrick shrugged. "All right, Grady. I'll take the call in my office."

He led Wentworth up to the main floor, where his office was located. As they entered, Kirkpatrick's secretary was bending over the short wave radio, tuning in to the police broadcast from upstairs in the radio room:

"Car Sixteen, go to Canton Importing Company Warehouse, under Brooklyn Bridge. Three-alarm fire reported—"

The phone rang at that moment, and Kirkpatrick waved his secretary aside, took the call himself. "Commissioner Kirkpatrick speaking!" he announced. He listened for a moment, then said crisply: "I'll be right over there!" and hung up.

"Come on, Dick!" he shouted. "That was the precinct house calling. The patrolman on the beat reported that several Chinese were seen escaping from the Canton Importing Company warehouse building, where that fire is raging. The patrolman said he saw a man in a wheel chair being carried into a sedan down the block, too!"

Wentworth's eyes gleamed. "Let's go, Kirk!" he exclaimed.

Police Headquarters is less than three minutes' run from the Brooklyn Bridge, with sirens working. Kirkpatrick's chauffeur drove up to the waterfront, where they could see the flames pouring from the four-story building of the Canton Importing Company.

Crowds were massed at the police lines, and fire engines filled the street. Hoses were pouring their streams of water into the structure, which gave every evidence of being about to cave in. Ladders were thrown up against the front wall, and firemen accoutered in gas masks and fireproof overcoats were mounting the ladders, axes in hand. A sweating fire chief was issuing swift orders to his men, and an ambulance stood near by, with first aid and with inhalators, ready for the first casualty.

The police lines opened before Commissioner Kirkpatrick's car. Kirkpatrick said to Wentworth: "Looks like a total loss, Dick. If it *has* anything to do with the Man from Singapore, and if there are any clues in there, they'll be entirely destroyed. This isn't going to do us much good—"

He stopped talking as Wentworth uttered a sharp exclamation.

"What's up, Dick?"

"There! See that man walking away from the waterfront—right over there, passing that policeman!"

Kirkpatrick stared. "Who—"

"That's Nils Bishop, Kirk—the man who was with young Custer in Mow Loo Fen's!"

"The hell you say! Here—let's get him—"

"No, no, Kirk! Don't you see? This is the break we've been waiting for. Bishop is tied into this thing in some way, of course. If you arrest him, he may not talk any more than those Chinese did, down at headquarters. Instead of that, I'll tail him, see where he goes, what he does!"

The broad figure of Nils Bishop was moving fast down the street, and Wentworth did not wait any longer.

"So long, Kirk!" he exclaimed, and leaped from the car, set off after Bishop.

It was at precisely this moment that the police, three blocks south of the fire, were fishing two exhausted, half drowned girls from the river.

And it was also at this time that Ram Singh and Jackson were receiving a telephone call, which was followed almost at once by two unexpected visits.

RICHARD WENTWORTH'S duplex penthouse apartment was located in one of the fashionable side streets in the Eighties, just off Central Park West. His only companions in that apartment were his Great Dane, Apollo, Jenkyns the butler, Jackson the chauffeur, and last but far from least, Ram Singh, his Sikh servant.

Ram Singh was a tall bearded man who struck terror into children at first sight, but whom they loved when they knew him better. He came of a long line of Sikh warrior kings, and pride of race was the strongest emotion he felt—next to a blind, loyal devotion to Richard Wentworth.

He sat in his master's music room on the upper floor of the duplex. His chair was near the window, with the telephone close to his elbow. He was moodily staring out through the open French window, which led on to the terraced lawn, covering most of the roof of the building.

The window faced south, but by looking to the right or the left, Ram Singh could see for miles in either direction, either across the East River toward Queens, or across the Hudson toward the Palisades of Jersey. To the south, he could see the flare of fire somewhere near the Brooklyn Bridge, but he paid no particular attention to it.

In fact, he was not interested in anything but the possible ringing of that telephone. Vainly, at his master's instruction, he had sat here for hours, in the hope that Nita van Sloan might call up.

As he sat there, he played absently with a long, bone-handled knife, which he had taken from a sheath under his belt. That knife was Ram Singh's favorite weapon, and there was a solemn oath enshrouding it. The Sikh warrior had inherited the weapon from his father, who had received it from his father before him. And the oath that went with the knife was as follows: that once drawn, it must not be sheathed until it had tasted an enemy's blood. Such an oath was not lightly to be regarded. To violate it would destroy a warrior's self-respect.

And now, Ram Singh was in trouble. So upset had he been by his enforced inactivity at the telephone, and by worry over Nita, that he had unconsciously drawn the knife and begun to flip it in the air by the blade.

Behind Ram Singh, at the other side of the room, Apollo, the powerful, intelligent Great Dane, sat before the fireplace, its eyes following the motions of the glittering blade as it spun through the air to be caught dexterously between the Sikh's thumb and forefinger. Ram Singh never missed, and one would almost have thought that the expression on the dog's face was one of disappointment each time that the knife was safely caught.

Jackson, the chauffeur, was striding up and down the room impatiently, nervously. From time to time he threw an exasperated glance at the Sikh. At last, unable longer to contain himself, he burst out.

"Damn it, Ram Singh, put that knife away! Can't you find anything else to do but juggle knives at a time like this?"

Ram Singh sighed, stopped flipping the knife. "I am sorry, my friend," he said humbly. "In a thoughtless moment, I drew the knife. Now I cannot replace it until it has bitten into the flesh of an enemy."

Jackson became contrite. "Don't mind me, Ram Singh, old man." He came over and put a hand on his fellow servant's shoulder. "I know how you feel. Juggle the knife if you want. Do anything—"

He paused, as the telephone began to ring.

RAM SINGH'S dark eyes gleamed, and his lips parted in a smile, showing straight, white teeth under his beard.

"Perhaps it is the *memsahib*—"

"I hope so!" Jackson exclaimed fervently, and snatched up the instrument.

"Hello!" he called.

His face fell, and he shook his head to Ram Singh, while he listened to the shrill female voice at the other end: "Let me talk to Richard Wentworth!"

"He is not in, madam," Jackson said. "Is there anything—"

"Who is this?"

"This is the chauffeur, madam."

"Well, give this message to Richard Wentworth as soon as you can. Tell him that he must come to see the flower woman."

"The flower woman?"

"Yes. Kate, the Flower Woman. He'll remember me. He was to come and see me tomorrow, but tomorrow will be too late. He must come before six in the morning. And tell him for God's sake not to fail me!"

"Does he know where to go, madam?"

"Yes. In the house behind Sin Foo's *lychee* nut shop, on the third floor. The door with the circle on it."

"I'll tell him, madam."

Jackson hung up, looked at Ram Singh. "It's the woman whom Mr. Wentworth met at Mow Loo Fen's. She wants him to come before six in the morning, or it'll be too late. What'll we do if we don't hear from him?"

Ram Singh shrugged. "I will go in the master's place if we do not hear from him. Perhaps it is a trap."

They both tensed as the sound of the opening elevator came to them from across the lawn. Some one was coming up. The entire apartment house was owned by Wentworth, and it was completely staffed by World War veterans who had served with him. These men were dependable and loyal, and it was certain that no one would be brought up who did not pass the keen scrutiny of the doorman.

Ram Singh and Jackson watched the tall, slender young man who crossed the lawn from the elevator. As he came closer, Jackson exclaimed under his breath: "Ram Singh! I must be seeing things! That man is the living image of young Martin Custer, who was killed tonight at Mow Loo Fen's! Either that, or it's his ghost!"

Ram Singh chuckled. "If it is a ghost, it must be a very cautious ghost, for it carries a gun. See the bulge under its armpit?"

Jackson nodded, and Apollo, rearing on his haunches near the fireplace, growled deep in his throat. The chauffeur muttered under his breath. "I could swear this is Martin Custer!" He stepped out on the terrace, looked down at the young man, watched him step up to the door of the apartment, down below. A moment later he heard the bell ring, heard Jenkyns, the butler, admitting him.

Almost at once the phone rang. It was Jenkyns, from the switchboard in the lower floor. "A Mr. Custer, to see Mr. Wentworth, Jackson. He says it's very important. Insists on waiting."

"Send him up," Jackson told him. Then he hung up, swung to Ram Singh. "See, I was right! It's Mr. Custer! My God—I never believed in ghosts—"

Ram Singh got up. "I have never yet looked upon a ghost that wore shoes, and carried a gun. It is in my mind to try whether this blade of mine will draw blood from it. Ghost or no ghost, I like him not. His face is callow, but cruel!"

Jackson was already on the way out. "I'll talk to him in the library, Ram Singh. Switch in the dictograph, and listen to the conversation. Perhaps you had better make a record of it, to prove that a ghost can talk."

Jackson's mouth twitched at the corners. He was quite startled at the resemblance of this visitor to the young man who had been murdered only a few hours ago, but he was amused at the seriousness with which Ram Singh denied he believed in ghosts.

He left the room while Ram Singh was kneeling beside the dictograph, cunningly concealed in what purported to be a wall safe, behind the piano. Ram Singh adjusted a pair of ear-phones on his head, then switched in an auxiliary needle which would make a record upon a wax roll of whatever would be said in the library.

Ram Singh, left alone in the room, winked at Apollo, then grinned. "Let us hear what Jackson's ghost has to say," he told the dog.

Apollo only yawned.

THROUGH HIS ear-phones Ram Singh heard the opening and shutting of the library door, then he heard voices:

Jackson: "You wanted to see Mr. Wentworth?"

Visitor: (hoarsely) "Yes, yes. I must see him at once. Tell me—where is he?"

Jackson: "I'm sorry, sir, but I can't tell you that. Perhaps I can help you."

Visitor: "My name is Custer. It's—it's a matter of life and death—"

Jackson: "Pardon me, sir, if I ask a question. I'm almost sure that I saw you, earlier tonight, entering the Eating Place of Mow Loo Fen—"

Custer: "No, no. That was my brother, Martin. I'm John Custer. We were twins—I was born seven minutes after Martin."

Jackson: (relievedly) "I'm glad to hear that—I mean, that's all right, sir. For a while, I—I thought—"

97

Custer: "You were seeing ghosts? It was hard to tell us apart. But see here—I must talk to Mr. Wentworth. It's about my poor brother, and the girl, Laura Gay. My brother is dead, and I've sworn to avenge his murder. There's a certain Doctor Sunderson who knows a good deal about Martin's death. I heard he was coming to see Mr. Wentworth, and I want to talk to him. Has he been here?"

Jackson: "No, sir, no one has been here." (Pause) "How did you hear that Sunderson was coming?"

Custer: "Never mind how. I know it. Now, look here. I know Sunderson was coming here. I want him. Will you take me to him? You see, I mean business!"

Jackson: "Why, Mr. Custer! *That's a gun you're pointing at me!*"

Custer: (venomously) "You're damn right, it's a gun! And I'll use it, too! Now, quick—take me to Sunderson!"

Ram Singh had not waited to hear more. He ripped the ear-phones off his head, and raced across the room toward the hall. That Custer should actually be threatening Jackson with a gun was almost unbelievable. The man's voice had sounded fairly normal, and there had been no hint of his producing a gun. But Jackson's words had left no room for doubt. He had spoken them deliberately so that Ram Singh would know what was happening.

And Ram Singh smiled through his beard, as he ran, gripping his knife. Here was a chance to wet the blade, so that he could return it to its sheath!

The door of the library was closed, and Ram Singh could hear nothing through the soundproofed walls. He put his hand cautiously on the knob, turned it very carefully, and pushed the door a fraction of an inch.

Custer's voice came to him, speaking with a new note of brittle menace.

"Your life means nothing to me, Jackson. I want Sunderson, and I want him badly—"

"You're crazy!" Jackson's voice came through the narrow opening. "I tell you Sunderson isn't here. Put that gun away, you fool—"

"I don't believe you, Jackson. I'm going to shoot in one minute—"

Ram Singh kicked the door all the way open, sprang into the room. He saw Jackson and Custer standing in the center, Custer only about three feet from the chauffeur. Custer whirled as Ram Singh came at him with the knife flashing. The Sikh displayed a fine disregard for the gun, his teeth flashing in a laugh of pure joy.

Custer shouted: "Stand back, damn you, or I'll shoot—"

He got no farther. Ram Singh and the chauffeur acted with splendid teamwork. While the Sikh held Custer's attention, Jackson sprang at him, struck down his gun wrist. The gun exploded into the floor, and then Ram Singh was upon him.

Custer fought madly, clawing, slugging, trying to get another shot. But Ram Singh had gripped Custer's gun hand with his left, while with his right he drove down against Custer's throat with his knife. Custer desperately held on to Ram Singh's knife wrist, trying to keep the thirsty point from his throat. But his strength was as a child's against the Sikh's. Slowly the blade came down, slowly and inexorably, until it was pricking the skin of the young man's throat.

JACKSON DID not interfere. He saw that Ram Singh had control of the situation, and he knew that the Sikh would not kill without reason.

Finally just as a single drop of blood spurted where the knife pricked Custer's throat, Ram Singh laughed with satisfaction, jerked the blade away. At the same time he twisted the gun out of Custer's hand, sent the young man spinning across the room with a mighty shove.

Custer tripped backward, landed on the floor, staring up stupidly at the bearded Sikh.

Jackson said quietly: "Well done, Ram Singh. You saved my life. The fool is excited about Sunderson's whereabouts. He would have killed me—"

He paused, looking quizzically at Custer, who had buried his head in his arms, and was sobbing.

"Hell!" he exclaimed disgustedly. "That's no way for a he-man killer to act. Imagine that, Ram Singh—a minute ago he was trying to kill me, and now he's bawling!"

Ram Singh shrugged. The Sikh was busily engaged in wiping off his knife. "Hah!" he said through his beard, in Hindustani. "Now I can sheath thee once again, faithful blade. Even though the blood thou hast tasted was but a drop, yet have I lived up to the oath which I took. Next time I promise thee a whole bucketful of blood!"

Jackson made a wry face. "Why don't you marry the damned knife?" he asked caustically.

Ram Singh raised his eyebrows. "You speak foolishness, Jackson. I have never heard that a man could wed a knife. Even in the *Rig-veda*, the Sacred Book of the Hindus, there is no reference—"

Jackson threw up his hands in despair. "All right, all right! I give up!" He went over to Custer, who was still on the floor, sobbing.

Custer raised his head, staring up at the chauffeur with reddened eyes. "Forgive me!" he blurted. "I lost my head. I made a mistake to threaten you—"

"Sure, sure!" Jackson scowled at him. "Just a little mistake like wanting to kill me! Do you go around making a lot of mistakes like that? Hell, didn't anyone ever tell you it hurts to get shot?"

"I was beside myself with anxiety!" Custer hurried on, getting to his feet. "Don't you see, I love Laura Gay as much as my brother Martin did. Her mother disappeared many years ago, when the three of us were children, and my father took her in to live with us. I've loved her for years, and when I heard what happened tonight, I couldn't stand the thought of her being in the hands of those Chinese. Then, when Mr. Bishop told me that Doctor Sunderson knew things about her whereabouts, and was coming here—"

"Wait a minute!" Jackson exclaimed tightly. "Did you say— *Bishop?*"

Custer nodded. "Nils Bishop. We knew him by sight at the house, because he came to visit my father once in a while. I knew that he had gone out with Martin earlier in the evening, but I didn't know it had to do with Laura Gay. You see, Laura had left us a couple of weeks ago, without saying where she was going."

Jackson glanced at Ram Singh puzzledly, then said to Custer: "Just a minute. You say Laura Gay left? Why?"

John Custer shifted uneasily. "You see, both John and I had asked her to marry us. She left a note behind, saying that she couldn't marry either of us, and that she was going off on her own, and for us not to try to find her. But we didn't obey her request. Both Martin and I were looking for her. Well—" he sighed deeply, lowering his eyes—"Martin found her first—and died for it!"

"This gets thicker and thicker!" Jackson grumbled. "What did Nils Bishop have to do with it?"

"I don't know—except that he used to carry out odd commissions in the Orient for father, and maybe Martin hired him to look for Laura. Anyway, Bishop called me tonight, and said that if I'd give him a thousand dollars, he'd give me information about her. I took the money out of the wall safe, and met him about two hours ago. He said that a certain Doctor Sunderson could tell me where to find her, and that Sunderson would probably call at this place tonight. He said if I came here and insisted on seeing the doctor, I'd find Laura."

Custer clutched Jackson's sleeve. "Please! Let me talk to Doctor Sunderson!"

Jackson frowned. "My God, don't start that again. I tell you, Sunderson's not here!"

Custer sighed. "Mr. Bishop told me you'd deny he was here."

Ram Singh suddenly laughed. "This Mr. Bishop—he knows

more than these humble servants of Mr. Wentworth. If this doctor that he speaks of is here, it is without our knowledge. We two, and the butler below, are the only three in this apartment!"

"I believe you now," Custer said. His shoulders drooped dejectedly. "And I don't know what to do. I'm as far from finding Laura as I was before I paid Bishop the thousand dollars."

"I think," Ram Singh growled, "that you should seek more information about this Bishop. Could you not ask your father about him?"

"No. My father's been out of town for almost ten days. He's visiting our Canadian mines. I expect him back by the end of the week."

Jackson winked at Ram Singh. "Tell you what you do, Custer. Let my friend with the beard take you into one of the bedrooms. Lie down and try to get some sleep. When Mr. Wentworth returns, he'll be able to help you. In the meantime, you get some rest."

Ram Singh gave Jackson the gun he had taken away from Custer, and took the young man by the arm. "Come," he said. "I will give you some hot rum, which is good for settling the stomach of those who have trouble. Then you can rest."

Custer allowed himself to be led out, without protest. All the starch seemed to have gone out of him.

Jackson, left alone in the room, stared thoughtfully into space for a while. He was trying to find the key to the jigsaw puzzle of events which had taken place tonight. There was no logical explanation for Nils Bishop's actions, and there did not seem to be any rational connection between Laura Gay and the Man from Singapore. Why should a beautiful young woman, who had led a sheltered existence as the ward of a wealthy man, suddenly leave to become a dancer in a Chinese restaurant, and bear the mark of the yellow fangs upon her breast? And why should the Man from Singapore have killed Martin Custer when that young man discovered the mark?

His train of thought was interrupted by the ringing of the extension telephone. There was an instrument in every room in this house, and Jenkyns from the switchboard downstairs could follow them around from room to room on a call.

Jackson hurried to the phone, anticipating a call from Wentworth. He was disappointed. It was Jenkyns.

"There's a man down here, Jackson," the butler announced. "He wants to see Mr. Wentworth badly. Says his name is Sunderson—Doctor Sunderson!"

CHAPTER 7
SIGNALS BY NIGHT

WHEN RICHARD WENTWORTH leaped out of Commissioner Kirkpatrick's car to set off after Nils Bishop, he had no idea where the trail would lead him. The mere presence of a man of Bishop's unsavory reputation in the neighborhood of the fire in the Canton Importing Company warehouse would have been enough to indicate some connection between him and the events of the evening.

Bishop's actions in the Eating Place of Mow Loo Fen had been highly peculiar. He had certainly guided young Custer there for the purpose of showing him Laura Gay. That he should have stood there and laughed unrestrainedly at the sight of his companion being shot to death was not inconsistent with what Wentworth knew of the ex-spy's character, to a certain degree. He knew that Bishop was innately sadistic, that he was the type of man who could find enjoyment in the sight of human suffering.

But Wentworth also knew that Bishop never did anything that would not yield a profit; and what profit could Bishop have hoped to make from the death of Martin Custer? If he had conspired with the Man from Singapore to lure the young man to his death, they need not have staged so elaborate a setting for the killing.

Rather, the way the thing had happened, Wentworth guessed that the shot had been fired only as a last resort, to prevent Custer from forcing further revelations out of Laura Gay. After the police raid on the Eating Place of Mow Loo Fen, both Bishop and Laura had disappeared. The question was, whether they had both disappeared independently, or whether Bishop had kidnaped the girl in the darkness.

Bishop's actions now were far from suspicious. The ex-spy walked rapidly westward, until he reached the Bowery.

Wentworth trailed about a half block behind him, crossing over to the other side of the street, so as not to attract his attention. At first it seemed that Bishop was heading toward Chinatown, and Wentworth tingled with the expectation of discovering Bishop's connection with this upheaval among the yellow residents of the district.

But instead of crossing the Bowery toward Chinatown, Bishop hailed a cruising taxicab. Wentworth glanced hastily around, saw that there was no other cab in sight. The ex-spy would surely get away.

Wentworth's lips tightened. He had not trailed this man only to be left standing here at the corner, helpless to follow. Boldly, he crossed the street, pulling his hat brim low. Bishop was standing at the curb, and as his cab pulled up, the ex-spy leaned over to get in.

Wentworth moved up close, paused, as if to light a cigarette. He heard Bishop say to the driver: "Go down to the Shipping Board Building on Bowling Green."

Wentworth moved on hastily, and Bishop's cab pulled away, made a complete turn on the Bowery, heading south. Still there was no other cab in sight. As Bishop's taxi gathered speed down the street, Wentworth strained his eyes for another, that he could follow in. Two cabs passed, but both had fares. By the time an unoccupied one came along, Bishop's car was out of sight.

Wentworth got into the taxi, clipped out to the driver: "I want to get to the Shipping Board Building on Bowling Green—and I want to get there fast. There's twenty dollars in it for you if you catch up with a cab that left here about three minutes ago!"

The driver nodded eagerly. "Consider it done, mister!"

Almost before Wentworth had closed the door, the cab spurted away. He was thrown back against the seat as the elevator pillars began to flash by with almost express train speed. The driver was determined to earn that twenty dollars!

Wentworth glanced at his wrist watch. It was four-fifteen!

The thunder of his automatics mingled with the bark of the machine guns.

He found it hard to realize that it had been only nine o'clock of the evening before when Charlie Wing's body had come hurtling down out of the sky to thud at his feet. That was only a little more than seven hours ago, and yet so much had happened! Men had died violently, hideously. A whole dreadful vista of conspiracy had been opened up before him. And his dream of sailing with Nita toward the quiet of a world cruise had been shattered.

Nita! The thought of her had been to the forefront of his mind for hours now. He had no doubt that she was in the hands of the Man from Singapore. If the Man from Singapore knew that she was a friend of the Spider's, it would go badly with her. And he had no doubt that this *was* known.

Somewhere here in the city was a secret headquarters, where Nita must be a captive. Perhaps she was even now in that flaming inferno back there at the warehouse of the Canton Importing Company. And instead of searching for her there, he was speeding down the Bowery, trailing Bishop.

Yet this was where he belonged. Bishop might be the key to the mystery, the answer to the problem of the motive behind the murderous operations of the Man from Singapore. And the fact that the ex-spy was going to the Shipping Board Building at four o'clock in the morning was interesting in itself.

WENTWORTH GLANCED out of the window. They were approaching Park Row. Traffic lights were off now, would not go into operation again until six-thirty, so that the driver could make all the time he wanted, with no stops. And he was surely making time!

Wentworth turned on the radio in the cab, tuned in on Station WLEF, which operated twenty-four hours a day for the benefit of taxi drivers, night watchmen, and others who had to remain awake while normal people slept. He was just in time to hear the announcer:

"Folks, we're all a little sleepy up here at the studio, but this news flash that just came in is strong enough to snap the sleep out of all of us! A mass execution of Chinese took place less than twenty minutes ago, in Chinatown. Fifteen members of the yellow race were found stabbed to death in the cellar of a house in Doyers Street. Each of the fifteen was marked with a peculiar scar upon his cheek—a scar that looks exactly like the fang marks of a wild beast.

"This happened while Commissioner Kirkpatrick was busy at a fire at the warehouse of the Canton Importing Company, on the waterfront. The fire is still raging, and the building is about to collapse at any moment. So far, not a single person has been taken out. Firemen and police do not know whether the building is empty, or whether people are trapped there, doomed to death in the flames. Hangers-on in the neighborhood report that the building was apparently occupied at all hours, for they claim to have seen automobiles arrive during the night and early morning. It is also stated that motor-boats have been seen tying up at the landing in the rear of the warehouse."

The voice of the announcer was interrupted for a moment, then he went on, a little more tensely:

"A bulletin has just come in from the police department. It has just been learned that the leaders of two of the most important tongs in Chinatown have been holding a joint, all-night meeting, and finally decided to go to the police with a problem of theirs. That problem is the mystery of the kidnaping of more than a hundred influential members of their respective tongs, in all sections of the country. These kidnappings have taken place in Albany, Chicago, Philadelphia, San Francisco, and other cities. In each case, the leading Chinese citizen in that town was the one who disappeared.

"Until tonight the tong leaders here were trying to meet this threat to the safety of their members in the traditional Oriental way, without the interference of the white agencies of law-enforcement. But the situation has now gotten beyond their control, and they have appealed for police protection. They state definitely that the mysterious Man from Singapore is behind these abductions, as he has been behind the unexplained murders that have been occurring with startling regularity. They fear that the Man from Singapore has reduced the Chinese population of the country to such a state of terror that he could easily force them to name him their absolute ruler, and to pay him tribute. As a matter of fact, collections have been started among the Chinese in many cities, with a view to gathering a large sum of money with which to appease the Man from Singapore.

"The tong leaders gave out this statement to newspaper reporters at headquarters, while waiting for the return of Commissioner Kirkpatrick from the fire at the Canton Importing Company Warehouse. They also said that in the last few weeks there has been an influx into the country of strange

Chinese, who have been doing the actual killing and kidnaping, obeying implicitly the orders of the Man from Singapore, even at the risk of their lives.

"The Mayor has been notified of the situation, and is hurrying to headquarters to take personal charge. He called the Governor of the State, and got the Governor out of bed in order to discuss the matter. What was said between the two officials has not yet been disclosed, but it is assumed that the Mayor asked the Governor for militia—"

WENTWORTH'S CAB had swung into lower Broadway, and now he caught sight of the red tail-lights of a taxicab about three blocks ahead of them. He switched off the radio.

"I think that's it!" he told his driver. "Take it easy, now. I don't want him to know he's being trailed!"

The few remaining blocks were covered with the lights of the cab ahead always in sight. As they swung into Bowling Green, Wentworth saw Bishop's cab pulled up at the curb before the Shipping Board Building, saw Bishop on the sidewalk, paying off the driver.

"Slow up," Wentworth ordered his man. "Pass that building slowly!"

He reached through the opening between himself and the driver's seat, handed the man two ten-dollar bills. "Here's your money. You earned it."

He descended from the cab, hurried back toward the Shipping Board Building, from which Bishop's cab had already departed.

He stepped up to the glass doors of the building. They were

closed, and locked. Evidently Bishop had been admitted by the night watchman, and the doors locked once more.

Wentworth peered in, saw the huge figure of Bishop entering one of the elevators at the rear of the lobby. Quickly, Wentworth stepped aside, so that Bishop would not see him when he turned around in the cage. He waited a moment, then stepped back to the doors. The elevator was rising, and he watched the indicator, saw it stop at the nineteenth floor. Swiftly he produced his skeleton keys, tried one after another until the tumblers of the lock clicked. He pushed the glass doors open, strode into the lobby.

The indicator was moving down again, and Wentworth hurried across to the bulletin board, ran his eye up and down, seeking those names listed on the nineteenth floor. At once a single name caught his attention:

Custer Gold Refining Company—1942

He felt his blood racing. This was better than he had hoped!

He swung around, saw that the indicator was at the second floor. In a moment the elevator would be down. At the opposite side of the lobby was the open door of a porter's room, and he could see a cot there, with a blanket thrown carelessly over it. That must be where the night watchman lay down for a cat nap during the small hours of the morning, when there was little doing. In the rear of the lobby was a row of telephone pay station booths, for the use of visitors to the building.

Wentworth darted to these booths, slipped into one of them just as the elevator reached the main floor. The bulb in the booth went on when he closed the door, and he reached up, unscrewed it. He waited, breathlessly, hoping that the watchman would not make his rounds now.

He was fortunate. After a moment he tiptoed out, peered around the elevator bank. He saw the watchman getting back into his bunk. The man was going to take another nap.

Wentworth nodded silently to himself, stole back to the telephone booth. He wanted to make a call, but he dared not insert a nickel in the slot, for the ringing bell that accompanied the insertion of a coin into a telephone box would surely be heard by the watchman.

Swiftly, he extracted from an inner pocket, a small kit of tools, packed in a flat, compact leather carrying case.

It was the screwdriver that Wentworth made use of now. He unscrewed the front plate of the telephone box, reached in with the pincers and snipped two wires. Then he used a small pair of pliers from his kit, holding the four ends of the two wires together, all touching. The handles of the pliers were thoroughly insulated, so that he could not get a shock.

By holding those four ends together, he created a short circuit that actuated the signal in the telephone company central office. Still holding the wires together, he picked the receiver off the hook, and was rewarded by the drone of the dial tone. He had his connection—noiselessly.

He dialed the number of his apartment, and in a moment he had the butler.

"Jenkyns!" he said tightly. "Quick, connect me with Ram Singh!"

Jenkyns exclaimed: "Thank God, Mr. Wentworth! Ram Singh

and Jackson have been worried at not hearing from you. There's news for you!"

The old man had been in Wentworth's service long enough to know when his master was under pressure. He wasted no time in gossip. Even while he talked he was ringing the upstairs apartment, and at once Jackson's voice cut in on the line.

"Mr. Wentworth! God, I'm glad to hear from you! I have several reports, sir!"

"First, take these instructions. Tell Ram Singh I want him. Let him take the limousine, and drive as fast as he can, down to the Shipping Board Building, on Bowling Green. He's to park about fifty feet from the building, and wait for me. I've followed Nils Bishop here, and he's up on the nineteenth floor, where the offices of the Custer Gold Refining Company are located."

"I see, sir," said Jackson. "If you'll hold the wire a moment. I'll give Ram Singh your instructions. He's right here."

Wentworth waited, and in a very short time, Jackson was back on the phone. "Ram Singh is leaving now, sir. He'll be there in a jiffy."

"Your reports, Jackson—swiftly."

"First, sir, there was a telephone call at three-twenty this morning. It was from a woman who called herself Kate the Flower Woman. She stated that you had promised to go to see her in the house behind the *lychee* nut shop of Sin Foo. Her room is on the third floor, and the door is marked with a circle."

"Right."

"She says that you must call before six o'clock in the morning, or it will be too late. That was all."

"Right, Jackson. I'll make every effort to go. But if I should be detained in any way, I want you to go in my place. She claims to have information about the Man from Singapore. You will hold yourself in readiness, a few minutes before six. If I find I can make it, I'll phone you. Otherwise, not hearing from me by a quarter of six, you will go in my place. Interview the woman, get all the information you can."

"I understand, sir."

"Next report!"

"At three-thirty, sir, a young man called here. He bears a marked resemblance to the murdered Martin Custer, and he gave his name as John Custer. He threatened with a gun, demanding that I let him talk to Doctor Sunderson, who, he claimed, was here in the apartment. He would certainly have shot me if Ram Singh had not entered in the nick of time. We disarmed him, and placed him in one of the guest rooms, under lock and key."

Jackson went on, telling Wentworth concisely what John Custer had told himself and Ram Singh. "It seems, sir," he ended, "that this young man is frantic with worry about Laura Gay, the dancer. And it also seems that Bishop knows Sunderson, for he was correct in informing Custer that the doctor would come here."

"Correct? You mean Sunderson really came?"

"Yes, sir. At three-fifty Doctor Sunderson arrived. He seems to be in a great state of fear, and cannot wait to talk to you. He will not say a word to Ram Singh or myself. We have him in the music room, guarded by Apollo. Neither he nor John Custer knows of the presence of the other."

"Good, Jackson. Things give promise of breaking—and they'd better break quickly. Jackson—" Wentworth's knuckles whitened on the receiver, while he asked—"has there been any word from Miss Nita?"

"Not a word, sir. I—I'm really worried."

"So am I, Jackson. God grant that she's safe. And now, ring off!"

He hung up, breaking the connection, tiptoed to the elevator, closed the door carefully, and started the car up.

He went up to the twentieth floor, intending to walk down to the nineteenth, so as not to give the alarm to Bishop, or anybody else who might be there. He found that the elevator here was close to a side window in the hall, and merely threw it a glance as he turned to find the stairway.

But that single glance was enough to halt him.

The window was partly open, and he could see that the building was set back here, at the nineteenth floor, thus forming a narrow terrace in front of the offices on the floor below.

And leaning over the terrace, out of one of those windows, was a man with a powerful flashlight, which he was clicking on and off, like a heliograph!

It was too dark to see the man's features, and he held the flashlight far above his head, so that it did not illuminate his features.

Wentworth's eyes narrowed, and he tried to follow the streaks of light from the flash, endeavoring to ascertain what code the man was using. It was certainly not Morse, and after a moment

Wentworth decided that it must be some prearranged code using flashes in series to convey coded phrases.

Swiftly he got out pencil and paper, and noted the sequences of flashes. Later on, with hours of study, he might be able to work out the key to this code, and transcribe the message. But there was no telling how long it would take to do that.

The man with the flashlight at last finished his message. But he did not withdraw from the window. Instead, he remained there, as if waiting for a reply.

With narrowed eyes Wentworth turned to look in the direction in which the man below was facing. The Shipping Board Building being located close to the southern tip of Manhattan Island, afforded a gorgeous view of the Upper Bay.

From where he stood, Wentworth could see the riding lights of numerous boats anchored in the Upper Bay. And abruptly, from one of them, off the Staten Island shore, he saw the flash of a night heliograph signal!

The ship was replying to the message from the man on the floor below!

Wentworth automatically marked down the flashes, and noted out of the corner of his eye that the man on the nineteenth floor was doing the same.

The message was a short one, and was over quickly. Wentworth kept his eyes on the ship, trying to fix its location in his mind. He drew an imaginary line through the boat; that line ran at an angle, from the mouth of Kill Van Kull, across the tip of Staten Island, to Fort Slocum on the east. Mentally he also noted the relative position of other vessels in the Bay. He should be able to find that ship with little difficulty, in the morning—provided it did not leave before then.

He was about to move away from the window, when he was startled by a hoarse shout from below. He tensed, glancing down.

The man with the flashlight was being attacked from the rear!

A dark figure had an arm around his throat from behind, and the two were scuffling desperately. The attacker had some sort of bludgeon in one hand, with which he was trying to strike the signaler, who was shouting some startled words in Cantonese. The words were unintelligible to Wentworth, above, and he did not wait to try to interpret them.

He swung around, leaped into the elevator, and slammed the door shut, pulled over the lever. At the floor below he brought the cage to a jarring stop, tore open the door, and leaped out.

The corridor ended here, as it did on the upper floor, due to the set-back in the building. Wentworth had to race around a bend in the hall to reach the office where he had seen the men struggling. There had been no light in that office, but Wentworth was not looking for lights; he was looking for number 1942, the office of the Custer Gold Refining Company.

Number 1950 had a light, but he passed it without stopping, for he knew by its location that it was not the room where the fight was taking place.

Further down, number 1942 was still dark, and no sounds of fighting came from it. Wentworth tried the door, found it unlocked. He took out his pencil flashlight and his gun, kicked the door open, and leaped in.

He brought up short, staring at the limp figure of a man,

who lay on the floor near the window, on his face. A long knife protruded from the man's back, and blood was rapidly spreading on the cloth of his coat.

Wentworth sprang to the man's side, played his light on the face.

It was Nils Bishop!

CHAPTER 8
INTO THIN AIR

B ISHOP WAS done for. His face was contorted in agony, and blood was bubbling at his lips. The blade had been driven to the hilt into his back, at such an angle that it must be piercing the heart. How the man managed to continue to live was a mystery. He was mumbling something through his bloody lips, and Wentworth bent low to catch the words.

"Orient—City—" he was saying—"Sunderson... get—the Spider... Kate—the Spider... the Spider... the Spi...."

His voice trailed off into nothing, a rattle sounded in his throat, and he stiffened. He was dead.

Wentworth got to his feet, with Bishop's last words ringing in his ears. *Orient City—Sunderson—get the Spider—Kate.*

It was a hodge-podge of words, spoken in desperation by a dying man. Were they the key to the mystery of the night? Did they name the Man from Singapore? Had Bishop meant that Doctor Sunderson was the Man from Singapore? Kate, the Flower Woman, had told Wentworth that she could give him

119

information—and now her name was mentioned through the bloody lips of a man who had just been stabbed to death.

Bishop's right hand, rapidly stiffening in *rigor mortis,* still held the leather-thonged blackjack with which he had made his attack upon the man with the flashlight. The signaler had called out in Chinese—for help, no doubt. And the help had come. Some one had come up behind Bishop while he was struggling with the other, and had expertly driven the knife into the ex-spy's back.

Then they had fled.

But where?

Wentworth had encountered nobody in the hall. He glanced swiftly around the dark office, sending his flashlight beam probing into corners. In the wall at the left there was a door, slightly ajar. That way, the signaler and Bishop's killer must have gone.

Wentworth glanced down, saw a small, leather-covered notebook on the floor at his feet. Automatically, he bent and picked it up, dropped it in his pocket. He might have looked at it then, but for the fact that he heard the shuffle of stealthy footsteps on the other side of the door in the side wall.

Some one was coming back!

The situation was clear to him now. The killer and the man who had signaled with the flashlight, perhaps others too, had not fled along the corridor, but through these adjoining offices. That room where he had seen the light—that was where they had gone. Then, they had come out into the corridor while he was here stooping over Bishop, had made their way around the bend to ring for the elevator—and had found the cage at their floor. They would understand at once that some one must have come up to investigate the fight in 1942. They would be returning now, to take care of that person.

Wentworth's gun was out. He doused his flashlight. In the darkness, he could distinguish the padding of more than one pair of feet. They must know he was here, for they must have seen his light. They would also know that he had heard them, by the fact that he had clicked off his own flash.

Wentworth did not wait for the attack. He moved stealthily to the corridor door, pulled it open. At once he realized his mistake. These men were no fools. They had taken care of the corridor too.

A wave of yellow men crowded into the room from the corridor, knives flashing. At the same time, there was another influx of Chinese from the adjoining room.

GRUNTED WORDS and high-pitched phrases filled the air as the two groups pressed against Wentworth. He fought silently, an automatic in each hand now, lashing out at the massed figures surrounding him.

He had one advantage, in that they were fighting in the dark. But the weight of numbers was with them. Blades stabbed at him from every direction, and he warded them off with difficulty, taking a bad cut on the back of his right hand from one of them who came in too fast.

He worked backward, away from the doors, and the Chinese spread out in front of him at a grunted command from one of their number. Knives were raised to throw. The Chinese hatchet-man can throw a knife with deadly accuracy, and appar-

121

ently their leader wanted to end this as fast as possible. Because Wentworth had not fired his guns as yet, they thought he was unarmed, and therefore spread out in front of him. It was sound strategy in so far as fighting in the dark was concerned, for it gave them a chance to distinguish their enemy. In the close infighting, some of them had been slashed by the blades of their friends.

But the strategy of spreading out was a mistake in this instance. Before the raised knives could be hurled, Wentworth's two automatics were barking out their grim message of death. Yellow men fell under the smashing impact of slugs fired with deadly accuracy at such close range.

Screams of pain and rage filled the air, mingled with the deep-throated roar of the guns. If they had hoped to accomplish this attack silently, they were disappointed.

Wentworth gave them no second opportunity to hurl their blades. He turned, leaped over the limp body of Nils Bishop, and vaulted the window ledge to the terrace, raced along it toward the office where he had seen the light.

Behind he heard yells and shouts as the surviving Chinese climbed on to the terrace after him. He reached the lighted office, peered in. The window was wide open, and the office was empty.

Wentworth turned, sent a single shot at the pursuing yellow men—a shot that served to slow them up while he jumped in through the window.

He sprang across to the corridor door, which was wide open. As he passed through he noted the inscription on the plate glass:

SCOURGE OF THE YELLOW FANGS

CANTON IMPORTING CO., LTD.
Importers of
Chinese Objects of Art
Ahmed Kupra-Sing
President

He had no time to give thought to that name, beyond connecting it momentarily in his mind with the burning warehouse on the waterfront. Some of the Chinese had raced back through 1942, into the corridor, and they saw him, raised a shout. Knives flashed in the air once more. Wentworth sent another shot at them, that reverberated in the corridor with the intensity of a twelve-inch mortar. The explosion was deafening—far more so than inside the office. The Chinese halted, screeching, and Wentworth ran down the corridor, turned the corner.

He made for the elevator, and stopped, lips tightly compressed. The cage had been moved. The indicator showed it to be at the roof, just above the twenty-sixth floor. Some one from those offices had gone up there!

WENTWORTH COULD hear the yelling Chinese coming after him, around the bend in the corridor. They would be here in an instant. He had no desire to engage in battle again with these hired hatchet men, while their chief escaped. The stairway was just a few feet past the elevator bank, and he reached it in a single bound, slipped through the doorway just as the first of the Chinese rounded the bend.

This was a fire exit, with iron stairs leading up and down, in a shaft outside the building. Wentworth slipped the catch on the heavy fireproof door before slamming it. Then he fired a shot into the lock. That shot jammed the lock, thus preventing pursuit by the Chinese. They would not be able to leave the floor until another elevator came up for them, or until the cage at the roof came down.

He started up the iron stairs, heading for the roof. He intended to find whoever was up there; and something told him that when he found that person, he would be close to the Man from Singapore.

He had not taken a half-dozen steps up, when he heard a sharp, *whirring* noise from above. He stopped, looking up. One side of the air shaft was completely open, and he could see the roof, six floors above.

He knew before he looked, what was causing that *whirring* noise. A huge black object rose into the sky, ascending almost perpendicularly, overhead.

It was an autogiro.

Wide, revolving vanes *whirred* in swiftly accelerating horizontal motion to lift the plane into the air. And Wentworth noted that the ship was equipped with pontoons—a seaplane with autogiro attachment!

As he watched, the plane swung into forward motion, headed south over the bay.

Wentworth's lips compressed tightly. There was no use going up to the roof now. His man had flown—literally. He watched the ship move out into the night, saw its black shape soar over the Bay, then saw it begin to descend—*toward the spot where shone the riding lights of the ship he had noted before!*

Tight-lipped, he turned away. The clamor of the Chinese behind the fire door had died down. They must have given up hope of breaking through after him. They must realize, too, that their leader had deserted them, left them to be found here eventually by the police. With characteristic Oriental fatalism, they were probably resigning themselves to whatever fate awaited them.

Wentworth turned, and ran swiftly down past the landing, to the floor below. He tried the fire-door here, found it locked on the inside. His skeleton keys had the simple lock open in a moment, and he was in the corridor of the eighteenth floor.

He glanced along the elevator bank here. The indicators showed all the cars except the one he had used to be at the main floor. He had no desire to ring for the night watchman and explain to that worthy what he was doing here at this time of the morning. Once the watchman was awakened he would undoubtedly go to the roof first, to find who had used the cage while he slept. He might even call the policeman on the beat to investigate. Wentworth had too many things to do to risk spending hours of explanation.

He got out his tool kit, attached a strong metal hook to the expanding metal rod. He then joined together three sections of the rod, until it was long enough to slip in between the sliding elevator doors of the shaft next to the one he had previously used. The hook caught in the bar of the catch on the other side of the door, and Wentworth lifted. The catch raised, and the door slid open, exposing the empty elevator shaft, with the cable running down the middle.

Wentworth looked down into the deep well of the shaft. Down there, eighteen floors below, was the roof of the cage. A failing body would be smashed to a pulp—far more effectively than had Charlie Wing's body.

Wentworth slipped on a pair of thin pigskin gloves which had previously been treated with a chemical solution to toughen them. These were gloves usually worn by him when he went forth as the Spider, and they were to come in handy now. He poised for an instant at the edge of the shaft, then leaped out into space.

His gloved hands caught the cable, gripped it hard, while he twined his feet around it. Then he slowly allowed himself to slide down. As his speed increased, his coat was whipped up about his shoulders, and he felt the rushing air billowing out his trouser legs. The friction was burning at his trousers and gloves. He relaxed the grip of his legs, pressed the arches of his shoes against the cable, still retaining the grip with his hands.

He was sliding downward at incredible speed, and he had no way to gauge his descent. Instinctively he tightened his grip on the cable, slowing himself up. He had acted not a moment too soon. The roof of the cage, at the main floor, was rushing up at him, not twenty feet below!

The effort of coming to a complete stop caused a terrific strain upon his arm and shoulder muscles, but he accomplished it less than three feet above the cage. Then he slowly lowered himself to the roof, sat down to catch his breath. He grinned ruefully at sight of his torn trouser legs, and the deep gouges in the sides of his shoes where the cable had scorched them. His gloves, too, had not withstood the strain. They were in shreds, and the palms of his hands were red and raw.

Once more he got out his tool kit, used the screwdriver to unfasten the trapdoor in the roof. Then he dropped into the cage, opened the door, and stepped out into the lobby. The loud snores of the night watchman testified to the soundproof qualities of the building. The man had heard nothing of the shooting upstairs.

QUICKLY, WENTWORTH tiptoed outside. As he had expected, Ram Singh was waiting for him with the limousine. The Sikh smiled broadly at sight of him.

"Your trousers, *sahib*—they look like the rags of the *untouchables* in Delhi. And your clothes are full of grease—"

"If you had just slid down eighteen floors of cable, Ram Singh," Wentworth snapped, "you'd look just as bad. Have I a change of clothes in the car?"

"Certainly, *sahib.*"

Wentworth got in, and at his direction Ram Singh drove the car around the block while he changed from a box of clothes and accessories under the rear seat. While he changed, he talked, telling the Sikh what had happened at the Shipping Board Building.

"And now," he went on, when he was attired in a gray business suit from the box, "I'll tell you what I want you to do. But first, let's see if there's any news."

He switched on the radio, got the police broadcast on the short wave. He stiffened, and Ram Singh in front tensed, as they heard the words of the police announcer:

127

"All cars! Watch for a sedan containing four Chinese. They are dangerous killers. Shoot on suspicion, but be careful of two girls who are prisoners of the Chinamen. The two girls were pulled out of the East River by a detail of patrolmen, not far from the fire at the Canton Importing Company warehouse. They are thought to be Miss Nita van Sloan and a dancer named Laura Gay. While they were being helped from the river, the four Chinese attacked the patrolmen helping the girls, killed all but one, and slugged Miss van Sloan and Laura Gay, dragging them into the sedan. The surviving patrolmen gave out a description of the Chinese before being taken to the hospital. Watch for a black sedan bearing District of Columbia license plates. It made off in a southerly direction, but all roads out of the city are to be watched. I will repeat...."

Bleak-eyed, Wentworth shut off the radio, stared at Ram Singh. "So the warehouse *was* the headquarters of the Man from Singapore! And Nita was his prisoner! She must have escaped with Laura Gay, and then those Chinese recaptured her!"

"What are we to do, *sahib?*" Ram Singh asked.

"Listen carefully. There's a ship out in the Narrows. Here's how it lies." Quickly, Wentworth drew a rough map on a sheet of paper from his notebook, showing the position of the boat he had observed in the Bay.

"I want you to go down to the Battery. Beg, borrow, buy or steal a launch. Go out in the bay and find that boat. Look her over, but don't board her. Then come back to shore and report to Jackson at the apartment. I'll be in touch with him."

"Do you know the name of the boat, *sahib?*"

"No—*wait!*" Wentworth snapped his fingers. The words of the dying Nils Bishop came back to him. "It may be the *Orient City*, Ram Singh. If it is, then we're on the right track. Don't waste time."

"Where do you go, *sahib?*"

"I'll take the car. I'm going to pay a visit to Kate, the Flower Woman. Then I'm going to the apartment and interview Custer and Sunderson—"

He stopped at sight of the pained expression on the Sikh's face.

"Your servant bows his head in shame, *sahib*. Sunderson and Custer escaped from us!"

"What?"

"It was thus, *sahib*. Sunderson called old Jenkyns, and asked to be taken to the men's room. When they were in the hall, he struck Jenkyns on the head, and took his keys. He must have known that Custer was in the place, for he searched for him, and unlocked the guest room where we held the young man. Then the two of them made their way out. It happened before you talked to Jackson, but he and I were in the library, and heard nothing."

Characteristically, Wentworth's first concern was with his servant. "Was Jenkyns badly hurt?" he demanded.

"No, *sahib*. It was a light blow on the head, and he is all right."

Wentworth sighed. Since the escape from the apartment had taken place before he talked with Jackson on the telephone, there would have been plenty of time for either Custer or Sunderson, or both, to get down to the Shipping Board Building. Either of them might have been the signaler with the flashlight.

He shrugged. "It can't be helped, Ram Singh. Now go ahead. It's only a few hundred feet to the Battery from here."

The Sikh bowed, got out and set off briskly toward the Battery. All the boats might be locked up down there, but Wentworth knew that Ram Singh would find some means of getting out to that boat in the Bay.

He himself drove north toward his rendezvous with Kate the Flower Woman....

CHAPTER 9
THE CHASE GROWS HOT

CHINATOWN WAS in a state of turmoil and commotion. As Wentworth drove through the narrow streets, he passed groups of police, who were patrolling the district in twos and threes. A police riot car was pulled up at the corner of the street where the Eating Place of Mow Loo Fen was located, and farther down the block Wentworth could see a large mob of people congregated in front of an alley. This must be where the mass execution had taken place. His car was stopped twice, and he was informed that all white people were forbidden to enter the district. In order to pass he was compelled each time to show his police card.

Finally he found it necessary to leave his car, and proceed for the rest of the distance on foot. Although it was barely more than five o'clock in the morning, the streets were full of yellow men, moving up and down furtively, glancing with suspicion at the white policemen. They knew that the battle between the police and the Man from Singapore was drawing to a head. They knew that their tong leaders had appealed to Commissioner Kirkpatrick; and they were awaiting the result of the momentous conflict.

Those inscrutable faces hid a good deal that Wentworth and the police would have given much to know. Wentworth was still in the dark as to the ultimate purpose of the Man from Singapore in inaugurating this reign of terror. He could not see how the mysterious personage hoped to gain by thus arousing the yellow men of America, by bringing the police at his heels. And he could not see the connection between the Custer Gold Refining Company and the Canton Importing Company.

He found the darkened store of Sin Foo, dealer in *lychee* nuts. There was an alley alongside the store, leading to the rear. Two plainclothes men were walking up the street. Further down, was the Eating Place of Mow Loo Fen, still under guard, and at the corner was the police riot car. If this was a trap for the Spider it would be an awkward time to spring it. Wentworth knew that his identity was known. He was fighting in the open, and if the Man from Singapore wanted to get the Spider, he had only to get Richard Wentworth; that had been demonstrated the night before. Now, Wentworth might be walking into another trap.

He shrugged, felt of his twin automatics, and stepped into the alley.

A slight tinge of dawn was reddening the sky as he stepped through the alley, out into the rear yard behind the store of Sin

Foo. The rear house loomed, dilapidated, dirty, slovenly. These places were common in Chinatown and in the poorer tenement districts. By putting up a place like this on excess land behind another house, the landlord was enabled to rent his rooms to almost destitute people at rents so low that they could afford them. Generally each room was rented separately, and the tenants were granted the privilege of cooking their miserable meals on a single burner gas stove, or on a charcoal stove. Such was the residence of Kate the Flower Woman.

Wentworth stood tensely at the mouth of the alley for a moment, surveying the rear house. There were no lights in any windows, but several of them were open, and he thought he discerned shadowy shapes in one or two of the first and second floor windows. He glanced straight up at the rear of the front house, and was almost sure that he detected a swift blur of motion as some one pulled in his head.

Wentworth smiled tightly. If this was a trap, he would walk into it with open eyes. His hands moved swiftly, up and down from his shoulder holsters, and palmed the two automatics. Then he dropped his hands to his sides. In the half light it would be difficult for anyone to tell that he was holding his two guns, with the safety catches off.

Now he threw back his shoulders, started to cross the rear yard toward the entrance of the dilapidated house. Almost at once, two figures appeared in two of the upper windows. At the same time, out of the corner of his eye, he caught sight of another figure at one of the rear windows of the front house. The ugly muzzles of sub-machine guns peered down at him. They were going to cut him down while he was crossing the yard!

Simultaneously, one of the sub-machine guns in the rear house opened up, spattering the flagstones of the yard. The gunner was wide of his mark. In a moment he would correct his aim. The *rat-tat-tat* of the machine guns crashed out in deadly rhythm, and bullets ricocheted from the flagstones, whined hungrily, and slapped the air close to Wentworth's ears.

HE STOOD stock still, with legs straddled far apart, and let go with both automatics, shooting with calm, deadly precision, before the gunners could move their sights to reach him. The thunder of his twin guns mingled with the staccato bark of the machine guns, and the back yard became a cauldron of deadly sound. But in a moment those machine guns ceased their chatter.

Wentworth had fired only three times, yet each shot told. One figure disappeared from a window of the rear house; the figure in the front house collapsed over the window sill; while the man in the upper floor of the rear house uttered a mad scream, toppled over, to fall, crashing, to the flagstones of the yard.

It was all over almost before it had begun. Echoes of the shots rumbled back into the sudden dreadful silence. Out in the street a police whistle sounded shrilly.

He mounted the stairs swiftly to the third floor. None of the occupants came out to see what had happened. These were all people who had learned through sad experience to shun trouble. Wentworth reached the third floor unopposed and unobserved.

He found the door marked with a circle in red crayon, and noted that the key was in the lock on the outside.

He holstered one gun, and with his free hand turned the key, pushed the door open.

Facing him, in the center of the room, stood Kate the Flower Woman, with a gun in her hand. There was an expression of utter hate in her old face.

For a moment Wentworth thought that she would shoot. But suddenly, as she caught sight of his face, she uttered a glad shout, and lowered her gun.

"Spider! You came through that trap! Glory be to God!"

"You wanted to see me," he said simply.

She nodded. "T—they found out that you were coming, and they locked me in here, set that trap outside. I was going to kill them when they came for me; I was hoping the Man from Singapore would come."

"You have something to tell me? Better hurry. I don't want to be found by the police."

"Then listen. Laura Gay is my daughter!"

Wentworth started.

The old woman saw it, and laughed. "You wonder how such a beautiful girl could be the daughter of an old crone like me? Well, I was once beautiful, too. But a devil got his clutches on me—the devil whom they call the Man from Singapore. He made me a dope addict. For shame, I disappeared, leaving my husband and my daughter. My husband loved me, and my disappearance grieved him. He went from bad to worse, and all the goodness went out of his heart. He wandered all over the world, an evil, bitter man. He became a spy, and out of his bitterness he betrayed all those he worked for."

"Bishop—was your husband?" Wentworth asked.

She stepped closer to him. "Did you say—*was?*"

He nodded. "Nils Bishop was killed a half hour ago—stabbed in the back."

Her shoulders sagged. "I knew he would end that way. The Man from Singapore got him. I—"

Wentworth gripped her shoulder hard. "Who is the Man from Singapore?"

She remained quiescent under his grip, looked up into his eyes. She paused, gulped, then: *"God help me, I don't know!"*

She went on, speaking in a low, fast monotone, while police whistles sounded outside, and men scurried about below.

"Nils Bishop knew. He knew who the Man from Singapore was. I could tell it in his eyes—that he knew—when he saw Laura that day last week, on the stage of Mow Loo Fen's, dancing, and when he knew that Mow Loo Fen had got his fangs into the girl, the way he got them into her mother many years ago. And I knew that Nils would try to avenge her. But I was afraid—afraid that Nils wasn't smart enough to fight the Man from Singapore. So I got Charlie Wing to appeal to the Spider for me. My mistake was that I took Sunderson into my confidence. Sunderson must have blabbed to the Man from Singapore. He would blab everything he knew if he was threatened with pain to his miserable body. They got Charlie Wing before he could see you. And they found out you were the Spider. Now they have Laura, and they have your girl, too. You'll be in the meshes of the Man from Singapore—"

"Wait!" Wentworth commanded. "I haven't much time. With what you have told me, and with what I've already discovered, I think I can put my hands on the Man from Singapore pretty soon. But tell me this—why does the Man from Singapore do all these things? What is his purpose?"

She laughed shrilly. "He aims to be emperor of all the yellow races in America. He carries on a big white slave trade with the Orient. He delivers girls to the brothels of the East. And he brings back Chinese hatchet-men who serve him faithfully. He has brought many men who could not remain in China because of the death laws for drug addicts. He smuggled them out of China, brought them here, and feeds them opium when they crave it. In return, they kill and murder and kidnap for Mm."

"I see," Wentworth said softly. "I promise you, Kate, that if harm has come to your daughter, she shall be avenged within an hour!"

Suddenly a mad light shone in her eyes. "They say—the Spider never makes a promise he can't fulfill. You—promise it?"

"I do!"

"Promise that you will never tell her about—her mother!"

"I promise!"

He left her there, standing straight, with the gun hanging at her side.

Downstairs, he peered out, saw that the police were gathered about the body of the dead machine gunner, while others were staring up at the front house from a window of which still hung the limp form of the man he had shot.

Wentworth made his way back through the creaking hall, found a rear door, and stole out. He went through an alley, out into the next street, then walked around the block and got into his car. Swiftly he drove out of Chinatown, found a telephone.

Jackson's voice was filled with eagerness. "Ram Singh called, sir. The name of the ship is the *Orient City*. It's manned by a Chinese crew. He's waiting for you at the Battery—with a launch!"

CHAPTER 10
THE ORIENT CITY

A MOTOR launch plowed through the swirling waters of the Bay, toward a ship anchored in the Narrows. The name of the boat showed on her prow in the growing light of the dawn: *Orient City*.

Ram Singh, at the engine, called to Wentworth: "That is she, *sahib*. There is no one on deck, and no one on the bridge. I saw no one when I was here earlier."

Wentworth nodded. "Pull around to the stern—"

He caught himself up short, staring at the two shadowy figures who had emerged on to the bridge. They were fairly close to the ship, and they could see that those two people were a man and a woman. They were running, hand in hand, peering behind them furtively, as if they feared pursuit. The man wore a dark alpaca coat like those affected by the Chinese, and a round coolie cap.

The two figures came to the rail, peered over the side, and the man seemed to be pointing something out to the woman. Wentworth noticed now that a rope was hanging over the rail, down to the waterline.

The two people on the deck seemed to be discussing something quite excitedly, and then the woman seemed to acquiesce.

Ram Singh looked inquiringly at Wentworth, who nodded. The Sikh got out a pair of oars, sculled the launch in under the tall ship, so that the end of the rope hung directly over them.

The two escaping people were down close to the boat now, but they had not yet discovered that they did not have a clear drop into the water. Wentworth heard the man say "I'm going to let go in a minute, Laura, dear. Are you sure you can swim all the way to land?"

Wentworth thrilled. This woman was Laura Gay! She was being aided to escape. But what had become of Nita?

He kept his voice very low, and called up to the two on the rope: "Don't be alarmed, you two. We are friends. Come down carefully!"

The girl uttered a frightened cry, and the man looked down. Wentworth saw his face, and gasped. He had never seen John Custer, but the man was the living image of Martin Custer, whom he had seen shot in the Eating Place of Mow Loo Fen.

Custer recognized Ram Singh, and called out: "My God! It's the Spider's man!"

"Come on down!" Wentworth ordered impatiently. "Do you think we have all day to exchange greetings?"

Custer slid down, dropped exhausted in the bottom of the boat, alongside Laura Gay.

Wentworth disregarded the young man, spoke to the girl: "Miss Gay! My name is Richard Wentworth."

She glanced up at him, smiled warmly. "Nita has told me all about you! She—"

"Where is she?" he demanded fiercely.

Laura Gay's face fell. "She's in the hold of the ship—with dozens of kidnaped Chinese. This is where the Man from Singapore keeps his kidnap victims. He's on board now—the Man from Singapore!"

RAM SINGH swore an oath in Hindustani. "The *memsahib* in the hold with the filthy Chinese! Let me get my hands on the throat of that Man from Singapore!"

"Wait!" Wentworth commanded him impatiently. He turned to Custer. "How did you two come to escape?"

Custer was shivering with the cold of the early morning. "Doctor Sunderson got me out of your place, promising to take me to Laura. He did. He brought me here, and he was as good as his word. But then the Man from Singapore came on board a while ago, and told Sunderson that he had been talking too much, and he just threw a knife at him, and the knife went into his throat! God!—" the young man shuddered. "I—I never saw a man killed before!"

"Never mind that!" Wentworth urged. "Go on with the story."

"Well, the Man from Singapore interviewed me, and for some

In that net was no baggage! Chinamen were tied hand

and foot, and above hung Nita Van Sloan.

unaccountable reason, he seemed to take a liking to me. He said no harm would come to me. He even gave me a cabin, off his own, and let Laura stay there too. We begged him to spare Miss van Sloan, but he wouldn't hear of it. He said that she was the friend of his greatest enemy."

Laura Gay broke in, going on with the story. "John and I decided that we couldn't let Miss van Sloan be murdered with all those Chinese—"

"Murdered?" Wentworth broke in.

"Yes. They're going to dump her and all the kidnaped Chinese into the ocean."

"Go on," Wentworth said bleakly.

"So we decided," Laura Gay continued, "to try to escape. John went out and found the rope, and hung it over the side, and then we stole out and climbed down—"

"You don't know," Wentworth asked young Custer, "why the Man from Singapore took a liking to you, do you?"

"I—I don't know. He seemed to treat me almost—almost as if—if he were doing it all for me!"

Wentworth reached a swift decision. "Take off your coat!" he ordered Custer.

The young man obeyed, and Wentworth took off his own, put on the Chinese coat and the coolie cap which Custer had worn. "All right, Ram Singh. Let's go. This is the last round!"

With the expertness of thorough training, the two men shinnied up the rope, leaving Custer and Laura Gay in the launch.

On the bridge, Wentworth saw that there was nobody in sight. But just as he started across toward the chart room where there was a light, he detected movement on the deck below. This was an old, weatherbeaten freighter, and there was the creak of a winch.

Wentworth glanced over the rail, saw that several deck hands were guiding the ropes of what must be a baggage net, coming up from the hold below, on the winch. The winch engineer was operating the gas engine which had set it in motion.

Wentworth put a hand on Ram Singh's arm, and the two men watched while the baggage net came in sight. Then they both uttered gasps of horrified amazement. In that net was no baggage!

Some two dozen Chinamen were gathered into that net like so many fish, tied hand and foot. And above them, to Wentworth's dismay, hung the limp figure of Nita van Sloan, hanging from the top of the ropes, by her wrists!

Wentworth's lips tightened, and his hand streaked to his holster, came out with an automatic. He was about to level it at the winch engineer, when there came a hoarse shout from the doorway of the chart room. Out of the corner of his eye Wentworth saw a wheel chair being pushed out on to the bridge. In that chair he saw the black-faced, hideous-featured Man from Singapore!

He leaped out of the chair, straight at Wentworth, while a uniformed figure who had appeared behind the wheel chair uttered stentorian commands in Cantonese to the crew on the deck below.

Wentworth fired at the winch engineer, hit the man in the stomach. The man screamed, and dropped, letting go of the lever.

Luckily, the winch was only about two feet above the deck, and the net dropped, without hurting Nita or the Chinese.

The Chinese crew rushed to the companion ladder leading to the bridge, and Ram Singh picked up a belaying pin, uttered a roar of pure fighting joy and went to meet them at the head of the ladder.

In the meantime, the Man from Singapore was clinging to Wentworth, both arms wrapped around his neck, trying to choke the life out of him, while the uniformed figure of the captain danced around in an effort to get in a blow.

Wentworth aimed a shrewd kick at the captain, caught him in the groin. The captain howled with agony, doubled over on the bridge. Wentworth backed toward the chartroom door, rammed into it hard, jolting the Man from Singapore, who was still clinging to his back.

Then he reached around, gripped one arm of the black-faced man, and pried it loose from his throat.

The Man from Singapore screeched, and clawed with long nails. Wentworth twisted the arm, elicited another screech, then swung around, pressing his opponent against the lintel of the chartroom door.

He had broken the man's hold on his throat.

Now he swung around completely, brought up a vicious smashing blow to the other's face. The man reeled backward, sprawled on the deck, his hand going to a holster under his coat. Wentworth watched him grimly, mercilessly, until he had the gun out. Then he deliberately shot the Man from Singapore through the heart!

The crew, attacking Ram Singh on the ladder, saw the Man from Singapore go down, and lost heart. They turned and ran, jumping over the rail like so many rats leaving a sinking ship.

Ram Singh leaped down to the deck, released Nita van Sloan from the net, brought her up on the bridge.

Wentworth was kneeling over the body of the Man from Singapore, gently scratching make-up from his face.

Nita uttered a gasp. "Then—he's not black!"

Wentworth laughed shortly. He went on peeling off the make-up, until the man's face was fully revealed. Nita exclaimed: "I've seen that face—"

"Of course you've seen that face!" Wentworth told her. "It's Frank Custer—the father of John and Martin Custer! It's he who was the Man from Singapore. It's he who has been carrying on this trade with China all these years, under the cover of a reputable firm name. No wonder he took a liking to John Custer. He wanted to make his son his heir—the heir to the greatest business in vice that the world has ever seen!"

Nita said softly: "Did he shoot his own son—back there at the Eating Place of Mow Loo Fen?"

"No. One of his gunmen shot Martin Custer, by mistake. The gunman did not know he was killing his master's son!"

Nita breathed a sigh of relief. "Then—it's all over—the terror of the Man from Singapore?"

"It's over, Nita dear," Wentworth told her. "And we needn't tell young Custer who he was. I—think the body can be buried—here, at sea!"

Five minutes later, just before a police launch arrived, a heavy

THE SPIDER

body went over the side of the ship—the opposite side from where young Custer and Laura Gay waited in the launch.

The body splashed. Wentworth spoke solemnly. "And so Kate the Flower Woman is at last avenged!"